Blue Heat

by

Samantha Cayto

Book One
Boston's Brave

This is a work of fiction. Names, characters, places, and incidents are either the product of the author's imagination or are used fictitiously, and any resemblance to actual persons living or dead, business establishments, events, or locales, is entirely coincidental.

Blue Heat

COPYRIGHT © 2014 by Samantha Cayto

Contact Information: info@thewildrosepress.com

Cover Art by *Diana Carlile*

The Wild Rose Press, Inc.
PO Box 708
Adams Basin, NY 14410-0708

Visit us at www.thewilderroses.com

Publishing History
First Scarlet Rose Edition, 2014
Print ISBN 978-1-62830-575-3
Digital ISBN 978-1-62830-574-6

Published in the United States of America

Welcome to the glamorous world of undercover…

Looking at Caruso, Finn realized he'd only ever been with boys before, teenage boys and college boys his own age.

Caruso was a man. The kind of man that could pick Finn up, hold him down, fill him up as he drilled him into the mattress.

A small noise escaped Finn's lips, a sound embarrassingly like a whimper.

The car jerked slightly as Caruso shot him a look. "You okay?"

"Ah, yeah." Oh, Christ, was that even his voice? He sounded like Mickey Mouse.

Caruso shot him another look, one that clearly conveyed his skepticism. Finn switched his gaze to look out the side window while he fought to get himself under control. His dick throbbed painfully in its cramped confines. Good enough for him. Having these thoughts about his boss while on the job was wrong. The last thing he needed was Caruso dumping him from the assignment because he was acting like a horny teenager instead of a displaced one.

It was a relief when Caruso finally pulled up in front of the Callaghan house. Finn had to look at him as he fumbled with the door handle. "I'll head over to South Station first thing." His voice no longer squeaked, but it had a breathless quality and it wasn't caused by the jeans he wore cutting off his circulation.

"Sounds good. Hey," Caruso added before Finn could push the door fully open. "You did great."

As he handed out the praise, his hand landed on Finn's thigh. The warmth of the large palm seeped through the worn denim and crept up Finn's leg right to his groin. Breath exploded out of his mouth as his cock stiffened even more. Then his gaze locked on Caruso's. Caught and mesmerized, Finn stared and stared some more. The amazing thing was that Caruso stared back. In the quiet of the car, the sound of their increasingly labored breathing engulfed them.

"I feel it, too," Caruso said finally in a low voice. "The attraction. I don't want to, and I tell myself to knock it the fuck off, but…"

Dedication

To all of the first responders in Boston.
We are Boston Strong!

Trademarks Acknowledgement

The author of this work of fiction
acknowledges the following trademarks:

Disney/Mickey Mouse: The Walt Disney Company
Escalade: General Motors
Keurig: Keurig Green Mountain, Inc.
Levi's: Levi Strauss & Co.
Mad Men: American Movie Classics Company
McDonalds: McDonald's Corporation
Midnight Cowboy: Bill Mack Country Inc.
Swiss Army Knife: Victorinox A.G. and Wenger S.A
YouTube: Google Inc.

Prologue

There was nothing more perfect than a summer night in Boston, warm with a slight sea breeze to keep the sizzling heat at bay. Rory Callaghan loved walking the streets of his city, especially when he had his pretty wife on his arm. Sheila was still a beauty in her middle years, only slightly rounder than she had been in their youth. But then so was he and without the reason of having carried and birthed three children, their sons.

Jesus, God, just the thought of his fine boys, healthy and strong, made his chest swell with pride. It was a bit sexist, yes, to be proud as a peacock that he had fathered three carbon copies of himself. He was a bit old-fashioned, so there it was. No fighting it. And each one of those boys was destined to wear the badge as he did, as his father and his grandfather and just about every other Callaghan male had for more than a hundred years since coming over during the famine.

It was a fine tradition to carry on even if times were dicey. There was trouble afoot, a rot in the force that came from top to bottom and back up again. It needed to stop before it infected many more. He hadn't thought he'd be the one to take charge, but fate had her way of grabbing a guy by the short hairs and making him take notice. He'd deal with it. He had to. The shield meant too much to him to turn a blind eye and let it all slide.

Tonight, though, was for his lovely bride of twenty-five years. He'd promised her a nice evening out, and he never went back on his word. Dinner had been expensive for a cop's salary, but she was more than worth it and had earned every morsel of pleasure he could give her.

Now, a nice turn around Columbus Park and the short drive back to their tidy house in Charlestown and maybe he'd get lucky. Luckier, of course. Any night he could lie beside the woman he loved, secure in knowing she was there and the boys were safely tucked in their own beds, was lucky enough for any man.

Squeezing her hand where it clasped his arm, he looked down at her and smiled. Still, a man could hope.

Except there was trouble looming in front of them. In a split second of time, everything changed. Hope turned to fear as the man approached. There was nothing to indicate danger other than the sense that twenty years of being a cop gave a man. He started to pull Sheila behind him even before the man showed his gun. Too slow. Damn it all, he was too late and too slow.

Sheila screamed when the first shot rang out. Rory pushed her down and flung himself at the man.

He didn't feel the first bullet or even the second, but his body seized and faltered and fell just the same. More shots and more screams. He twisted his neck to see his love and found her beautiful sightless eyes staring back at him.

No! God, no, it couldn't end this way. He'd failed to stop the rot and in that failure had thrown his woman into the danger. He'd trusted the wrong men or tipped his hand when he thought he'd been careful. Either way, it was over.

As he gazed up at his killer one last time, he thought of his boys. He would never see them wear the badge, wasn't sure they should if this was how it would end for them. God protect his brave boys.

Chapter One

Finn Callaghan jack-knifed up in bed, panting through the last of his nightmare. Beside his bed, his alarm screamed its way through his aching head. He slammed his palm on top of it without looking, a practiced move that silenced the damn thing.

Christ, he hadn't had the awful dream where he lived through his parents' murder through the eyes of his father in a long while. It didn't take a psych degree to understand why it had come back to plague him. Today was the day he followed the Callaghan tradition and pinned on the badge. Of course, he'd think of his father, the best cop he'd ever known. Rubbing the palms of his hands over his sweaty head, he tried to calm himself.

His bedroom door swung open after a perfunctory knock, and his brother, Daire, popped his head inside. "Oh, good, you're awake. Don't want to be late for your graduation."

"Seriously?" Finn rolled his eyes. "I've been getting myself up for years now. You don't have to mother hen me."

Daire leaned against the door jam and studied Finn with eyes that always saw too much, more than what Finn wanted them to see anyway. He was just like their father, which was why Daire was the second best cop Finn had ever known.

slender with light brown hair and wild eyes. He looked up at Michael and whimpered.

"Please don't hurt me," he begged in a rough and pleading voice. "I won't fight any more, I promise."

Slowing his steps, Michael held out his free hand in what he hoped was a soothing gesture. "It's okay. I'm not here to hurt you. I'm a cop. The whole place is filled with cops. You're safe. We're going to get you out."

Tears formed in the kids eyes. "You mean that?"

"Absolutely." Michal turned briefly to show the boy his back, where his jacket said Boston Police on it. "See?"

A sob tore out of the boy's mouth. "I can't go home. They don't want me there."

"It's okay. We'll find a safe place for you," Michael vowed and tried not to show how pissed he was, not just at the people who had taken advantage of this runaway, but also at the people who should have cared for the kid in the first place. He couldn't believe how parents could turn their kid out just because he was gay.

Washington popped his head in. "I've got four more boys down the hall." His gaze flicked briefly over to the kid, and Michael saw the same fury in his partner's eyes as he felt. God, vice sucked.

"Have them send the EMTs up as soon as things are under control down there. Every one of these boys needs to be taken to the hospital for evaluation."

"Roger that." His partner disappeared.

Michael turned to the boy, who lay shivering. "It's going to be okay." He holstered his gun and, pulling his jacket off, laid it over the kid.

He wanted to believe his own words, yet knew the sad truth was, things weren't okay for this boy or any of the others they'd found in this house of horrors. Maybe some of them would be able to go home. Not all of them had been kicked out for being gay or any other reason. Some of them had parents who were desperate for their son to be returned. No matter what, though, the recovery from this kind of abuse would take years, if not a lifetime.

In the meantime, this raid had netted some fish but not the big one. There was still someone out there running the ring that preyed on runaways and sold their bodies to as many men as they could find. Until Michael got the guy and brought him down, he'd be staring at a lot more terrified boys.

****

"Come on, give me bigger smiles."

Finn turned his lips up wider to please his uncle, Jack Malloy. He had his arms around his brothers, and their cousin, Regan Malloy, was on the other side of Ronan. All three of them were shiny in their uniforms, and he was proud to have them flank him.

Uncle Jack clicked a few times before lowering his camera. "That's fine, then. I'll have copies made big enough for framing."

"Wait, Dad, take a picture with my phone," Regan asked, holding it up to toss to her father.

Jack waved the notion away. "You know I can't deal with those things. I have what I need." So saying, he capped the camera lens and stuffed everything into the bag on his lap. Regan's father was confined to a wheelchair, thanks to a perp years back who'd pushed him down a flight of stairs. That didn't stop the guy from getting around, though, and Finn was touched he'd also shown up in his old uniform.

"Thank God," Daire said quietly. "I love you, little brother, but I hate having my picture taken." Daire slapped Finn on his back. "How about we head back home? Aunt Mary and the others have already left to get the food out."

Finn rolled his eyes. "Seriously, you don't have to go to so much trouble. It's not like I graduated high school or college." Even as he said it, he was secretly thrilled that so many of his family had come to graduation and were making such a fuss. He couldn't help looking down again at the metal pinned to his chest. He was so damned proud of being accepted onto the force. There was only one thing that would make this day better—two things, people.

He had to blink away the tears that sprang up all of a sudden. It was too much to hope his brother wouldn't notice.

Hugging him closer, Daire said into his ear, "They're here. I feel it."

Finn shot him a reassuring smile, although he wasn't so sure his brother was right. He'd tried so many times to detect the presence of his parents, had lain endlessly in his bed late at night trying to see, hear, or feel that some part of them remained. There had been nothing.

Still, he honored them as best he could with what he did with his life. Doing well in high school, getting into Boston College, the family alma mater, and now graduating from the Academy and joining the force— that was his way of keeping them close. And halfway through college, he'd also done the one thing he needed to do to be true to himself, the thing he couldn't do when they'd died. He'd come out.

"Come on," Ronan urged as he clamped his arms around Finn. "I'm starving. Let's go."

Before they could take a step toward the exit, the police commissioner strode up, his hand extended. All three of the Callaghan brothers stood up straight, and Finn took the proffered hand. Sean Finnegan was Finn's namesake and godfather and had been their father's best friend. It wasn't the same as having his actual father there, but it was a close second.

"Congratulations, Finn, my boy," the older man said, his big hand clasping Finn's firmly. "It's another proud day for the Callaghans and brought tears to my eyes to hear you speak of your father."

"Thank you, sir. I couldn't not mention him."

"Of course not. He was the finest man and best cop I knew. It makes no difference what some here might think. We know he was honorable."

"Yes, sir." Finn fought to keep the smile on his face. Although he couldn't see his brothers' expressions, he knew they were forcing themselves not to grimace. It was an infuriating fact that the rumors of his father being on the take and his parents being murdered in some kind of double cross of the so-called Irish mob wouldn't die. He knew both of his brothers hadn't given up trying to uncover the truth. He'd vowed to do the same now that he was a cop.

"Well, I'm sorry I won't be able to stop by for your party." The commissioner made a face. "I have to go to an event hosted by the mayor."

"I understand, sir. Thank you again for your good wishes."

Finnegan gave a wave and a nod to each of the brothers before striding off. Ronan made a rude noise under his breath.

"Political brownnoser."

"Ronan!" Daire admonished.

"It's true and you know it. He's never lifted a finger to clear Dad's name. Doesn't want any of the stink to rub off on him."

"Let it go," Daire ordered. "Today is Finn's day. We remember the happy and let the rest go for now."

"For now," Ronan agreed and, slapping Finn on his back, he said, "Food!"

Finn laughed because it was what his brothers wanted. But as he walked off with them, he silently agreed with Ronan. None of his father's friends on the force had wanted to look too hard at what had happened. They were afraid of either being painted by the same brush or of what they'd find. The Callaghan brothers weren't afraid of either thing. They knew their father hadn't been dirty, and they'd find the truth no matter where it led them.

****

Washington's sneeze was loud enough to envelop the lieutenant's tiny office. Michael stopped mid-sentence and glared at his partner.

"Sorry, man," Washington said through the wad of tissue up against his nose. "This damn cold keeps getting worse."

"Maybe it's allergies," Lieutenant Bates said. "They're wicked bad this time of year."

"Yeah, I don't think so, LT," Washington replied. "Feels like I've got a fever."

Michael blew out a frustrated breath. "Jesus

fucking Christ, can we get back to the raid?" His partner glared peevishly at him and nodded. "Anyway, LT, we've got the boys under the supervision of child protective services. We can't interview them until they've been medically cleared, then we need to make sure they have a lawyer present with a social worker or parents if we can get them here, and blah, blah, blah. Bottom line, we've got a bunch of traumatized minors and some low level pimps and enforcers from whom we've sweated as much information as we can, and we're still no closer to nailing the guy in charge than we were when we started."

"I thought your informer said the guy would be there."

Michael paced a circle in the small space. "That's what he said, and he's a reliable snitch. We found one room in that piece-of-crap house that didn't need to be fumigated. It was done up a little nicer than the other rooms and looked like it had been recently occupied, given the sheets were rumpled and warm. My guess is the asshole got tipped off and ran right before we got there."

"Leaving his people behind? Sounds stupid to me. Why aren't any of them rolling on him?"

Another loud sneeze from Washington startled Michael. He grimaced at his partner, who shrugged. The poor guy did look a little glassy-eyed and sweaty.

"Given that we've stumbled over more than one dead body in this investigation, I'm thinking they're too scared to give him up. And we certainly had our hands full with who we found, so if he had left recently, we didn't notice."

The lieutenant sighed and tipped his head back to

gaze at the ceiling. "Where exactly does this leave us?"

Michael took a second to marshal his thoughts. He'd been pondering his next move for hours. He thought he had an idea that would work. "I want to try sending someone in undercover."

"You mean have someone infiltrate the organization?"

"No, sir. It would take forever to get someone to a point of being trusted. This guy hasn't been successful by taking chances. I was thinking of getting someone in from the other end of the operation. According to the boys we've rescued, once a boy is considered to be 'broken,' if you will, cowed into submission and at least no longer fighting them, they may get sent to spend time with the top man. Apparently he likes to consume what he sells. He's picky, though. He takes only the best looking boys, and he never spends more than a night or two with one. Most of the time, he comes to them. Rumor has it, though, once in a while a boy is sent to him. We just haven't managed to find any of those boys or at least none that will admit to it."

"I'm not following you."

Michael licked his upper lip. "Have someone pose as a runaway and maneuver to get him recruited by one of the pimp's boys."

Bates stared at him for several seconds with eyebrows raised. "You're looking for a cop to pose as a teenage boy?"

"Yes, sir. We've done it before with high school drug stings. We just need someone who looks sixteen or so and attractive enough to catch his attention. This fucker preys on boys much younger, but some of them are close to twenty. As long as they look young enough to the johns, they keep them on the string."

Bates nodded. "Okay, I can see it. It's worth a try."

"Yeah, but there's one more thing, LT." A small knot of apprehension formed in Michael's stomach. This was the tricky part. He knew he was right, though. "We need to pick a rookie, someone not known to a lot of the detectives and uniforms."

Washington coughed hard, not as a commentary, however. It sounded like the cold had travelled to his lungs.

Michael looked at him and frowned. "Seriously, man, you need to go home or something."

"I'm fine," his partner said stubbornly.

"Why do you want a fresh face?" the lieutenant asked, then held up his hand. "Never mind, stupid question. You think someone in the department is on this pimp's payroll."

"Yes, sir, I do, and believe me, it pains me to say it."

"Crap," Bates muttered and heaved a big sigh. "I agree." He tapped a pen against the edge of his desk in obvious thought. "I think I've got the right guy. You know Sergeant Daire Callaghan?"

"By reputation, yes."

"Well, his youngest brother just graduated at the top of the Academy's class earlier today. I dropped by for the ceremony, because Daire and I were classmates. The kid, Finn, fits the bill perfectly. You'd swear he was seventeen, tops, and even a straight guy like me recognizes he's a looker."

Michael stiffened a fraction of a second at the mention of sexuality before relaxing again. He knew Bates didn't mean anything by it, even knowing

Michael's orientation. While Michael didn't exactly march in any parades, he wasn't completely in the closet, either.

"Sounds like our man," he said neutrally.

"I can't say he wouldn't be recognized after giving the graduating speech, but maybe if we let his hair grow a little and put him in the right clothes, even someone who had seen him might not recognize him."

"It's a risk we have to take. We have to use a cop for the role, and a rookie is our best bet."

"Okay, then, I'll call Daire and set up a meet between you and Finn. We'll do it at their house so no one sees it."

Standing up, Michael nodded. "Sounds good, LT. Thanks."

"Yes, sir, thanks," Washington added before bending over in a half sneeze, half cough.

"Jesus, Washington," the lieutenant said as he picked up the phone. "Caruso's right. Go home."

Chapter Two

Finn popped off the couch at the sound of the doorbell. It'd been hard to wait for the arrival of the men behind the front door. Although he understood the need for secrecy and meeting at night made sense, he'd been antsy all day. Well, at least all afternoon, given how late he'd slept in. His family had pulled out all of the stops with his graduation party, and enough beer had flown to give him a sore head and a sour stomach for the first few hours of the day. Those minor problems had faded into the background when Daire had revealed the call he'd gotten the previous night.

His brother hadn't wanted to weigh down the celebration with shoptalk, so he'd waited to talk to Finn until this morning. Finn understood the sentiment, but Jesus, this was such an exciting opportunity, he wouldn't have minded putting down his bottle of beer to hear it. He just wished Daire was as enthusiastic about the assignment as he. Of course, his brothers had always tried to talk him out of joining the force—a matter of "do what I say and not what I do." He'd politely told them to fuck off. He was a Callaghan as much as they were.

"This is dangerous undercover work," his brother had said earnestly over coffee several hours ago.

Finn hadn't even bothered to hide the eye-rolling. "No shit, Daire. Undercover police work is always dangerous, so is walking a beat or riding in a squad car. The whole damn job is dangerous."

"I know, don't remind me," Daire muttered. "You should have gone to law school."

"Yeah, 'cause that's what the world needs, more lawyers." He gave his brother a measured look. "Although if I got my law degree, I could parlay that into joining the FBI."

Daire grimaced. "Are you trying to make me throw up? Fed work is worse!"

"I know," Finn replied with an evil grin. "I'm just yanking your chain. I can't believe you're still trying to convince me to give up the profession I've worked so hard to enter. And successful undercover work will look great in my file and help me make detective sooner, hopefully."

"Right. Fuck." Daire rubbed his hand down his face. "This assignment requires you to pose as a gay teenage runaway."

"I got that. Seems like a perfect fit for me."

Daire winced. "That's what I'm afraid of, frankly."

On a groan, Finn rocked back in his chair. "Come on, bro. That's like telling an actor he shouldn't play a gay role, because everyone will think he's gay."

"Except you are gay."

"Yes, I am, and I'm not ashamed. I'm not hiding in the closet, you know."

"I do know. And I don't want you to be ashamed. You have nothing to be ashamed about. I don't want you hiding who you are, either."

"But?"

"But it's the force, and you know that even with people's views on this 'evolving,'" he said using finger quotes, "cops are still pretty macho, and I hate for you to have a sign on your back. I don't want you to be hassled."

Finn shook his head. He'd had some version of this conversation with both of his brothers since he'd finally come out to them and announced he would major in criminal justice with an eye to joining them on the force. He swore his two brothers worried more about him than all of the mothers in the world ever could.

"You're selling your fellow cops short. They're more open-minded than you give them credit for."

"Most are. It's the ones who aren't that I worry about. Like maybe this vice cop will figure if you're gay, you're expendable."

"Jesus, Daire! At least meet the guy before you paint him as a bigot."

The discussion had ended then, and by unspoken agreement, they'd steered clear of the topic for the rest of the day. Now, the vice cops were here and it was time to find out exactly what his role would be. He had to work to contain his excitement and appear cooler than he was.

Daire opened the front door, and a guy walked in wearing street clothes. He grabbed Finn's attention and held it in a headlock. Dark, wavy hair and olive-tinged skin. A little taller than his own five ten, the guy was jacked with broad shoulders and a narrow, tapered waist. His worn jeans molded around thighs like tree trunks. Finn felt kind of delicate in comparison, and even Daire, who was more filled out than he was, looked a bit puny. Brown, intelligent eyes swept the foyer and landed on Finn. There was a sizzle and pop in the few seconds their gazes locked before Daire broke the connection by sticking his hand in front of the guy.

"Caruso?"

"Ah, yeah. Michael," their guest said and shook the proffered hand. "This is my partner, Detective Sergeant Wayne Washington."

Finn forced his gaze past the sexy Caruso and saw an even larger man entering behind him. Washington was African American with a nose so noticeably red, he either had a serious drinking problem or a hideous cold. The man's greeting was obliterated by a large sneeze into the crook of his elbow.

Daire and Finn took a step back from the germ zone, but Caruso merely shook his head.

"Come in and sit down," Daire offered as he shut the door.

Finn turned back to the living room and placed himself by the couch, figuring he and his brother could sit there with the tempting Caruso and his infectious friend taking the wing chairs.

"Finn, right?"

Finn found those deep, dark eyes focused squarely on him once more. They were so warm and compelling, he could have stood there all night staring into them. But as a gay man living in a mostly straight world, he pulled himself together and shook the hand Caruso held out to him .

"Yes, sir. Officer Finn Callaghan as of yesterday afternoon."

"I heard you were at the top of your class," Caruso said, sitting down on one of the chairs.

"Yes, sir."

"He made his older brothers look bad," Daire said with a grin. "Ronan and I didn't graduate quite so high in our classes."

Finn felt his cheeks flush at the attention and the praise. It was like being a little kid and patted on the head for doing a good job. Daire and Caruso meant well, but he just wanted to get down to business. Everyone was seated, so time for serious talk.

"Sir, Daire told me you need someone undercover for a prostitution ring?"

Caruso grimaced. "Yeah, Wash and I have been working to nail this one pimp in particular. He runs a lot of boys, mostly underage and mostly runaways. He uses the usual con of having the boys he's already broken-in troll the bus and train stations, youth shelters, soup kitchens, and the like to convince vulnerable kids there is somewhere they can make good money and be independent. Once he's got them in one of his houses, he uses intimidation, beatings, rape, and drugs to get and keep the boys in line. If one of them O.D.s or a john gets too rough, we find their bodies in the Charles or dumpsters."

"Jesus," Daire said quietly. "Vice sucks. No offense."

"None taken," Caruso assured him. "My very thoughts every fucking day." He glared at Washington as the guy spent a few seconds hacking up a lung then turned back to Finn.

"We've been close, really close to getting this guy, but every time we think we've got him cornered, he slips through. We've taken out parts of his network, and of course, he just replaces them. There are always more goons, lackeys, and boys. We need to cut off the head."

"If we can find it," intoned Washington from behind his tissue.

"Right," Caruso agreed. "The really shitty part about all of this is, we think someone on the force has been warning this asshole so he gets away."

Daire swore, and jumping up, he paced away from the couch. "The fuck you say!"

"It pains me, it really does to think it, but my gut's telling me we have to play this close to the vest. That means other than the four of us, and a couple of tech guys I'd trust with my life, only my lieutenant will know about Finn being undercover."

"I trust Bates, and you'd better be right about the others," Daire warned.

"I'm as sure about them as I can be sure of anyone other than Wash or myself."

Finn tamped down his mounting nerves. This sounded dicier than he'd originally thought, although the opportunity was still too good to turn away. "Why me?"

Caruso turned his attention back to Finn, and the impact of those smoldering eyes hadn't diminished. Warmth spread through Finn's body and blood pooled in his groin. Okay, that was a problem. He didn't need the added trouble of a hard-on, especially in front of his overprotective brother.

"We need someone who can pass for mid-teens and who's not known well on the force in case I'm right about the snitch and he or she ends up running into our undercover officer." He shrugged his shoulders. "To increase the chance he can get somewhere close to the head pimp, our guy has to be attractive—cute, you know? Vulnerable-looking is a bonus." Caruso's gaze bore deep into Finn. "You fit the bill, kid."

Heat flared behind the cop's gaze that lasted for a

second, or maybe it was only Finn's imagination. Because it gave him all kinds of bad ideas, he lashed out. "I'm not a kid, sir, although I grant you I look like one. I get carded all the time."

"See," Caruso said with a smirk. "Just what we're looking for."

"So, how does this work with my current precinct assignment?"

"The official word is you caught mono and won't be able to start work for a few weeks."

Finn barked out a laugh. "Seriously? Mono? Did I catch it playing spin the bottle?"

Caruso treated him to a devastatingly cute smile, dimples cutting deeply on both sides. "I know it sounds cheesy, but you have to be out with something that takes weeks, not days to get over. Fever with mono often lasts for a couple of weeks, plus we've secured a letter from a doctor saying your spleen is enlarged and at risk of rupture. It puts you out of commission for about a month. We're hoping this assignment won't last that long. Once we've got our guy, your role will be revealed so you can get the recognition you deserve."

Washington took that moment to cough up his other lung.

"Would you like some tea or something?" Finn asked, because, Jesus, he needed a moment to process what was being offered to him.

"Don't go to any trouble," Washington wheezed.

"We have a Keurig. It's no trouble at all. Come take a look at the selection."

Finn got up and headed into the kitchen with the other cop in tow. He pulled out the tree of K-cups and waved his hand at them. "Daire likes tea." He made a face. If it wasn't coffee, Finn considered a hot drink to be a waste. "You have a few choices."

He made himself busy, rummaging around for a clean mug and mulling over what it was going to be like pretending to be a teenage runaway. He could grunge down and channel his high school self. What was going to happen once the ring picked him up, though? Was he expected to actually prostitute himself to gain the trust of the pimp's lackeys to get close to the big man? Could he even do something like that? His experience with other guys ran the gamut. He wasn't a virgin or anything. Still, he hadn't exactly been a slut in college, and training at the academy was intense enough that he'd put dating on hold for the duration.

He took the K-cup Washington had picked out and put it through the machine, the fog-horn sound it made while processing amusing him as it always did. Raised voices coming from the living room startled him.

"What the fuck kind of question is that?" Caruso shouted.

Finn glanced up at Washington, who only shrugged and took the mug of tea being offered. Finn trotted back to find his brother and the other cop squaring off. "What's going on?"

The two men didn't spare him a glance. "A legitimate one," Daire spat back. "He's my baby brother, Caruso, and I want to make sure he's covered."

"You insulting asshole! I've spent the better part of the last year rescuing runaway boys, lots of them gay, from being exploited, and you have the audacity to ask me if I'm going to leave your brother hanging out there just because he's gay?"

"Ah, shit," Finn muttered. "Come on, Daire, I leave

you for five seconds and you turn into a douche?"

"Stay out of this," his brother ordered with a jab of his finger. "I know what crap goes on out there." He rounded back to Caruso. "I'm not apologizing for the question, and I notice you haven't exactly answered it."

"Really?" Instead of backing down, Caruso put himself toe-to-toe with Daire. "How's this for an answer. Your brother's sexual orientation doesn't mean squat to me. I'm gay myself."

That shut Daire up. Washington shuffled up next to Finn, sipping his tea. He winked at Finn with one of his rheumy eyes. Long seconds ticked by. Caruso held Daire's gaze. Finally, Daire looked away.

"Well, all right then." He surprised Finn by coming over and clapping his hand on Finn's shoulder. "I support whatever decision you make." Then he looked at Washington. "Did my brother give you any whiskey to put in there?" When the cop shook his head, Daire said, "Come on. You need more than tea for that kind of cold."

Michael watched his partner shamble back to the kitchen in Daire Callaghan's wake. Christ, it was all he'd been able to do not to clock the guy after he asked the most insulting question he could imagine asking a fellow cop. As if he'd deliberately leave a brother hanging out to dry. He should have taken the swing. Instead, he'd blurted out something that was no one's goddamn business. His answer had really been for the younger Callaghan's benefit, though. He didn't want Finn to worry for one moment that Michael wouldn't protect him with his life if he had to.

Shoving his hands in his pockets, he took a moment to regain his composure. It wasn't just the confrontation with Callaghan senior, either, that had him rattled. The very presence of Finn unnerved him. Michael had said the guy fit the bill for the assignment, and that was no lie. It was the understated way he'd said it that was disingenuous. Finn looked young, yeah, so young the attraction Michael felt for him was uncomfortable, like robbing the cradle. Because he wasn't merely cute, he was exquisite with his black hair, blue eyes, and pale skin. He had a slight build, but his toned muscles were visible in his T-shirt and cargo shorts. Eminently fuckable, and when Michael matched those impulses to those of the guys he was trying to shut down, it made him a little nauseated.

Except Finn wasn't a kid. He was an adult and a cop and not a dating prospect. That little fact needed to be emphasized to his libido, which had been cooperatively dormant for the last few years. Why the fuck did it have to rouse now?

Michael cleared his throat and plunked down on the chair he'd sprung from when Daire started his interrogation. He kept his hands in his pockets even though it was awkward. He didn't trust his cock not to poke up more than it had already.

After a moment's hesitation, Finn returned to his seat on the sofa. "I'll do it," the guy said before Michael could even start the conversation back up.

"Are you sure?"

"Yes, sir." Finn's stare was steady, no hesitation, no doubt.

"All right. We'll take a week to familiarize you with what we know about the ring and its leader. It will give your hair a chance to grow some, but you'll need to keep shaving so you'll look younger."

"Got it."

"We should meet here at night where no one can see what we're doing. That is, if your brother doesn't mind and if he can keep his nose out of it."

Finn made a face, as if having his older brother poking into his affairs was an old pain in his ass, too. "Don't worry, I'll make sure Daire behaves."

"Good," Michael said, although he wasn't convinced it would be that easy. The Callaghans were probably like the Carusos—large, loud, and clannish. No way Finn's older brother would fade into the background. Plus, there was another older brother on the force. And wouldn't it make for a fun party if that one decided to show up? "Do you have any questions?"

Finn scrunched his face up in a way that made Michael want to kiss him. "Just one." The guy visibly swallowed. "There's no way they're going to pick me up and take me directly to the top man."

Michael shook his head, knowing where this was going. "No, they won't. The shithead likes his boys young, but he's careful about who he 'honors' with his attention."

"So, I'm going to have to be with them for a while to make them trust me. That means turning tricks, doesn't it?"

The topic deflated whatever happiness his cock had started to feel. Taking his hands out of his pockets, Michael ran them down his face. "I don't know. Maybe. Probably," he amended. "I was thinking you might be able to string them along for a few days, especially if you play it eager but shy. They won't necessarily force you right off if they think you'll be a willing participant given some time." He shook his head. "I could be way off base there. We can also send guys in to pose as johns, make it look like you're working."

He gave Finn a pointed look. "Bottom line is, we can't guarantee you won't be forced to do things you don't want to do. If that's a deal-breaker, I understand."

Finn was quiet for long seconds, staring at the back of his hands as they lay on the tops of his thighs. Then he sighed and looked at Michael once more. "It's not. I guess it's a good thing I am gay. While I don't want to have to service any johns for real, I know I can do it if push comes to shove."

"Your sexuality shouldn't play into this," Michael said vehemently. What Finn said didn't sit well with him.

"It shouldn't, but you and I both know it does, if only because I can't walk away from this knowing gay boys who've been kicked out by their families make up a big part of the victims."

"Okay, then." Michael stood up. Holding out his hand, his stomach did a little flip-flop at the idea of touching this man again. When Finn clasped him in a firm shake, the touch was to his cock what a lightning strike had been to Frankenstein. Desire was awakened from its too-long slumber, and it was hungry.

Their gazes locked, and in the clear blue of Finn's eyes, Michael could swear he saw the same need. The idea scared him enough that he yanked his hand free and bolted away.

"Washington, let's go," he called into the kitchen.

His partner looked even worse, if that were possible, but maybe a little happier courtesy of the nip in his tea.

"You need to get to bed, man," Michael said with a

shake of his head. "I'll see you tomorrow night at this time, Callaghan." He didn't dare look back as he steered his partner out the door.

****

The dingy room smelled like stale cum, the remnants of a hundred hurried and shameful couplings. Finn stared at the narrow bed covered in a wrinkled and stained sheet. That was where he needed to lie down and surrender the use of his body to the man standing behind him. He could hear the labored breath that came from mounting excitement, feel it even on the back of his head. Finn's heartbeat increased, forcing his own lungs to work harder. For him, though, it was fear that drove the quickened response. Or was it?

Large hands gripped his shoulders, squeezed once before sliding down his chest to cup his pecs. A harder squeeze made him gasp, then moan as thumbs circled his hardening nipples. Finn closed his eyes against the squalor of the room and leaned back against a hard chest. Warm breath tickled his ear.

"You like what Daddy does to you." The low, seductive voice held almost an accusation.

Finn rocked his head forward and shook it. "No, that's wrong. You're not my daddy, you're a rapist." He spit out the accusation even while his body betrayed him with his hard cock straining for release.

The arms around him tightened when he tried to break free. His captor chuckled. "It's just a game, my sweet Irish lad, just pretend. Come and play with me. I promise you'll like it."

"No," Finn murmured again but even to his own ears, his protest sounded feeble.

"Let me get these clothes off, and then you'll see

how good it can be."

In the next instant, Finn was naked. His dick stood out from his body and eager to play with this man who was totally forbidden, yet impossible to resist. He wasn't the only one, either. Now an equally naked body pressed against him. An enormously large and stiff rod rode the crack of Finn's ass. A shudder ran through him at the thought of what that monster could do to him, for him.

"See," the tempting voice crooned. "You like what I've got. You want it, don't you?"

Finn whimpered as he nodded. He didn't want to want what this man had. He couldn't help himself.

"Then I'll give it to you."

Finn's eyes popped open as the man shuffled him forward. He saw the disgusting bed and shook his head, dug in his heels. "No, not here. Not like this."

There was another chuckle against his ear. "Oh, does my pretty boy want a pretty place to fuck? Fine, then, anything for you."

The room around them shifted and morphed into a luxurious room, like something in a fine hotel. Now, the bed was huge and covered with crisp, clean, white sheets. Finn didn't resist as the man pushed him forward. In the blink of an eye, they were at the edge of the bed, and Finn was turned and all but tossed onto it. He knew even before he'd stopped bouncing on the firm mattress who he'd see when he looked up.

Michael Caruso loomed over him, every muscle in his large body on display. Dark hair sprinkled across his chest with a thin treasure trail ending at the base of that enormous cock. It jutted out from his body, all red and shiny from a steady drip of pre-cum. Finn swallowed hard.

Michael clasped the rod with one hand. "This is for you, pretty boy. You want it, don't you?"

Licking his lower lip, Finn nodded. He couldn't speak any more, only pant with anticipation and need. His own dick throbbed. He lifted his legs and spread them to expose his hole in invitation. Was he mad? Could he even take such a large cock without being torn apart? He didn't know and didn't care. He had to have it.

Michael growled and pounced like a predator, his big body slammed against Finn, covering him, smothering him. Finn bucked up instinctively against the assault, but there was nowhere to go. Michael had claimed him completely even before his lips pressed against Finn's and his tongue invaded Finn's mouth. Michael all but choked him as he swept every corner while his teeth scraped along Finn's lips. So complete was the conquering that Finn almost didn't notice the moment when Michael's cock breached his hole.

A burn, the likes of which Finn had never experienced, caused him to arch within Michael's embrace. Not wholly pain nor pleasure, it was a perfect blending of the two. His cry was muted by Michael's tongue. His struggles to get away from the assault or closer to it, he wasn't sure which, were in vain. Michael held him fast.

Breaking off the kiss, the man pressed his forehead against Finn's and whispered, "Don't fight me or yourself. You want this."

Finn tried to shake his head. "No, this is wrong. We shouldn't be doing it."

In response, Michael drove himself deeper into

Finn's body. Finn cried out again and rocked his hips to take the dick in farther. His cock was trapped between their bodies, and every time either of them moved, the friction jacked his pleasure.

"It's still wrong," he ground out, although who he was trying to convince, he didn't know.

Michael's teeth nipped at Finn's earlobe. "It's okay to be bad every once in a while, sweet boy. You don't always have to be good."

A different type of cry ripped past Finn's lips. "Yes, I do. My brothers have trouble enough. I can't give them more of it."

"Shh, it's okay." Michael's voice was soothing and seductive. "They're not here. This can't hurt them. It's only a dream."

"It feels so real."

"But it's not. You know it's not. Just lie back and enjoy it."

Then there were no more words, only a mouth claiming his once more and a cock thrusting into his body faster and harder. Finn's climax mounted with each stroke to his prostate and the friction against his dick. He tried to clasp it with his hand. The body on top of him blocked the way. Then it didn't matter because he was coming. He thrashed in time to the pulsing of the ropes of cum shooting out and splashing against his stomach.

With a gasp, Finn rocked up in his bed. He gulped in large breaths as his heart jackhammered in his chest. His body shuddered with aftershocks, and sweat coated his skin. With an unsteady hand, he touched the outside of his boxer briefs, sticky with the cooling remnants of his wet dream. He brought his fingers up and stared at them in the gloom of his bedroom.

Shit!

He'd taken psychology courses in college so he shouldn't be surprised at the turn his dream had taken. Worry about the undercover assignment coupled with an attraction to his new boss had equaled that same guy being a john in his subconscious fantasies. Simple and so very fucked up. How was he supposed to look the guy in the eye when they met to go over the task force's files? And how was he going to tamp down his attraction, especially now that he knew the other man was gay?

Wiping his hand against his thigh in disgust, Finn flopped back down. He'd find the strength to do it. He had to.

Chapter Three

"We don't even know the fucker's name."

Caruso was a liberal user of the various forms of "fuck" Finn came to understand within five minutes of sitting down with him. And as soon as the guy walked into the house, Finn had resolved to think of him by his last name. First names were for lovers, or for fantasies, and there'd be no more of that.

They were in the dining room with the pieces of the prostitution ring's file spread out on the surface of the old oak table Finn's mother had polished on a weekly basis. Finn could swear he still smelled the lemony scent as he sat hunched over the tabletop. It was both comforting to still be in the familiarity of his childhood home and also a constant irritation, like the scratching at an open wound.

"Those of his people we've managed to scoop up only refer to him as 'Boss.' Not 'the boss,' just 'Boss' like it's a name or something."

Perusing the various mug shots, Finn saw a variety of hard-looking men. They all had previous records, of course, and he wasn't surprised they were smart enough not to roll on this Boss character. Prison was hardly a safe place for informants, and while this ring was important to the Boston vice squad, it wasn't necessarily big enough to offer long-term witness protection.

Some of them were different, though. Younger men in their twenties with a sneer on their faces that tried to mask their underlying fear. These were likely victims who had survived their years of abuse and hardened to the point of making a lateral move in the organization to become one of the minders of the boys. He felt sorry for them and hoped they would be treated with more leniency even while he understood they might be too far gone to save.

Then there were the current victims. Leaning over, he made himself look at the photos of the dead boys and the beaten ones covered in blood and bruises. He reviewed every detail of the catalogue of injuries discovered by the doctors when the boys had been rescued. He gave them a few minutes of unflinching attention, so he could always picture in his mind the purpose of his undercover work. He might have been orphaned at a vulnerable age and had chosen to keep his sexuality a secret for a few more years. Yet, at the same time, he'd known if he came out to his family, he wouldn't be turned out, shunned, and left to fend for himself.

"If they know anything, they're too scared to say."

As soon as Caruso spoke, Finn realized how close he'd leaned toward the other man. Not good. He shifted back into his chair. "Were you able to question any of them at length?"

"Not really. Some of them were so traumatized the doctors have blocked us. A lot of them have left the state, gone back home." He picked up a photo of a slender boy with light brown hair and wary eyes. "This kid, Craig, is being housed by social services. He's from fucking Kansas, and his parents won't come and get him. They thought he was wicked even before they found out he'd been whored out to countless men."

"Assholes." Jesus, what else was there to say?

Caruso sighed. "Yeah. They hadn't had him long, though, and he was at the house we raided a few days ago, the one where Boss, the fucker, was supposed to be. The kid might have seen or heard something useful, so I'm going to go talk to him again tomorrow."

"Take it easy on him," Finn said, not thinking to sensor himself.

Caruso glared at him for a second, but before Finn could apologize for questioning the man's abilities, Caruso's expression softened. "I will. Don't worry. I've been working vice for about seven years, often dealing with kids like Craig."

They sat in silence for a few seconds, each of them pretending to look at the paperwork and not each other. At least, Finn was pretending. Thinking Caruso was doing the same was projection pure and simple. He might seem distracted, but the guy was not only a hardened and focused cop, he was older and more experienced. The likelihood he'd be attracted to a wet-behind-the-ears officer was low. He'd already said he thought Finn was cute, as if he were a puppy. Not the kind of lover a macho guy like Caruso would probably look for.

A pity. He was exactly the kind of man Finn had always been attracted to. Big, strong, overtly masculine, and older was a bonus. Someone who took charge. The type of man who always topped. Finn had tried that position once, and while it was pleasurable enough, it just wasn't him. He liked the sensation of having his body claimed by someone stronger. He wasn't a masochist or anything. Definitely a bottom, though.

The house was warm from the heat of the day, and although the night had cooled, they couldn't leave a window open for fear of being overheard. Frugal Daire had also decreed it wasn't hot enough to turn on the air conditioning. The proximity of Caruso's large body wafted heat toward Finn, making him uncomfortable and sweaty. Of course the effect was from more than mere temperature.

Finn was careful to keep his body flush to the table's edge to hide the obvious impact of his attraction. He forced himself not to fidget. At least his brothers had made themselves scarce before Caruso had shown up. If they'd been there to notice his discomfort, he wouldn't hear the end of it.

Caruso popped up suddenly and grabbed the briefcase he'd brought the material in. "Look, why don't you review all of this on your own tonight and tomorrow and make a list of questions." He held the case in front of him almost like a shield. "I'll be back tomorrow night, hopefully with Wash, to answer them."

"Oh, how's he doing?" He was so consumed by Caruso's presence, he hadn't thought to ask about his partner.

"Sick as a dog. For now, he's his wife's problem." Caruso grimaced. "He probably won't be well enough to come tomorrow." He said it as if he were really disappointed.

Was being alone with Finn that much of a burden? "Okay." He didn't know what else to say.

"Right, I'll let myself out."

Caruso turned to go, but before he'd taken more than a step in the direction of the front door, something inside Finn made him either stupid or crazy. "What's it like?" he blurted out.

Caruso paused and looked back at him. "What's what like?"

Finn lowered his gaze. "Being openly gay on the force."

Yeah, stupid and crazy, except Caruso had volunteered the information last night, even if it had been done out of temper. Despite the bravado he put on with his brothers, he was at least a little concerned about how other cops would treat him.

Caruso didn't answer right away. He stood there, chewing his lower lip in a way that made him look younger than he was. Finally, he answered, "I don't know that I'm the right person to ask. While I'm not exactly in the closet, I'm not very open about being gay, either." He took a deep breath. "My family doesn't know."

"Oh," was all Finn could think to say in response to that confession.

"None of them are cops, so my worlds are kind of kept separate. I wouldn't lie if any of them asked me directly about it, but they're kind of old world, you know? I don't think it would occur to them I'm gay." He shrugged. "Anyway, regarding the force, I've never been hassled by anyone. Of course, not many people mess with me."

"Wicked big as you are, I can imagine." As soon as the words were out of his mouth, Finn felt a blush creep up his face. At least, he knew better than to try to "fix" his observation by insisting he hadn't actually noticed or anything. Obviously he had.

"Ah, yeah, you got that right." Caruso's cheeks

looked a bit pink themselves. "I'll see you tomorrow."

With that, he was gone, leaving Finn sitting at his mother's beautiful table covered with crime scene photos and grisly reports. And yet his cock pressed painfully against his fly. It was going to be another tough night.

****

Michael had had one hell of a fucking awful night. Racing out of the Callaghan house like his dick was on fire hadn't helped one bit, either. His dreams had been filled with the delectable Finn, except every one of them had morphed into a nightmare in which Finn was a young boy being brutalized by faceless men while Michael tried in vain to reach him. Each time, he'd woken in a cold sweat only to fall back to sleep for the next horror show.

The worst of it was that even after such a crappy and scary night, he still had a hard-on for the guy. Adding to his worry? He was pretty sure the feeling was mutual. What a clusterfuck it would be if they actually acted on the attraction. As the senior man, it was his duty to make sure it didn't happen. Not only could it compromise the investigation, Michael was not on the market, as it were, not even for someone as appealing as Finn. Life was complicated enough without bringing sex into the picture, and a man like Finn deserved more than a one-night stand anyway. A guy like that screamed relationship, and Michael, for sure, didn't have that in him.

So he drowned himself in the strongest coffee he could find as he sat in his car, waiting for the clock to tell him it was time to go into DCF and interview Craig again. His gut told him there was more the kid knew that might prove useful. There was intelligence lurking behind those frightened eyes, and he was a fighter. The ring might have beat him down to a point of compliance, but there was strength there still. Michael was sure of it. Swigging the last of his cup, he got out of his car, locked up, and found a place to toss his trash.

He was cleared at the door and escorted to a small conference room to meet with Craig and the court appointed attorney there to protect the boy. As much as Michael understood the need to protect a minor, he also knew a boy wasn't as likely to open up about his abuse with a woman present. It was embarrassing enough to talk about sex with any adult. Doing so in front of a grown woman must feel like talking in front of your mother. The sad fact was that more women were willing to work in these caretaking careers with low pay than men, so they were stuck with Ms. Brown.

In she came, quietly cheerful and fresh enough out of law school to be truly optimistic. Craig slunk in behind her, head down, dressed in a long-sleeved shirt and jeans. The day was already turning too warm for the shirt, although Michael suspected the kid had preferred to be as covered as possible. His arms had to be peppered with fingerprint bruises and his wrists still ravaged by the ropes he'd been tied with.

"Good morning, Sergeant Caruso," Ms. Brown said as she held a chair out for Craig and sat in the one next to it.

Michael and Craig sat, too, although the boy mostly slouched down with his arms crossed. He didn't acknowledge Michael, and that was okay. Michael might have been the man to rescue him, but he was also the one who'd seen him at his worst, a frightened, naked sex slave.

"Good morning, Ms. Brown. Hey, Craig, how's it going?" When the boy only shrugged in response, the lawyer took up the conversational ball.

"How can we help you, Sergeant?"

Pulling out his small notepad and pen from his back pocket, Michael said, "I was hoping I could ask Craig some more questions about the men who held him. Maybe he's remembered more information that might be useful in rounding up the rest of the ring."

"They're rats," Craig said in a low voice.

Both adults looked at him, waiting for more. When none came, Michael pressed, "What makes you say that?"

So many seconds passed he was sure the boy wouldn't answer. "They scurry around the city. You can hear them, see bits of them sometimes, then they disappear again."

Michael leaned over the table, although not so much to be intimidating. Damn, it was hard to hide his excitement. He'd been right about this kid being both courageous and smart. A smart person would notice things even when afraid.

"They moved you around a lot you told me the last time." An almost imperceptible nod. "And they had different guys watching over you?" Again the nod, this one more emphatic.

This was as far as he'd gotten with the boy the last time he'd talked to him. Then he'd shut up, shaking, crying, and Michael had to stop the interview. No tears or shaking now, not yet. Brown watched both of them like a hawk, a mother one, ready to peck Michael's eyes out if he didn't take things easy.

"Okay, that's good, Craig, really helpful. Now, can you remember anyone's name?"

Again seconds ticked by, then a minute or two. Michael sat as still as he could, keeping his breathing steady and quiet. They had all the time in the world, or at least that's what he wanted Craig to feel. Brown, bless her, kept quiet, too. An ally after all so long as Michael didn't fuck things up.

A first name came tripping out on a stutter, then another. Seven names in all were given by the boy, and Michael wrote them all down even though he knew these names already. These were all men picked up on the raid. Then after a lull, a few more names came out, ones Michael didn't have. Those he noted with some relish, although with them being only first names, their immediate use wasn't obvious.

"Good," he said again, thinking it sounded stupid. "That's very helpful." Now for what he really wanted. "The night of the raid, there was a man in the house who you might have seen before but wouldn't have seen often. Did you see someone the others might have referred to as Boss?"

The boy drew in a sharp breath and let it out on a hard shudder. Brown made a move as if to put a soothing hand on Craig's shoulder. He shied away from the touch, almost falling off his chair. She snatched her hand back and grimaced at Michael.

"You don't have to answer any more questions if you don't want to," she said in a soothing voice.

The boy's knuckles showed white, he gripped his arms so tight. "I want to," he bit out. "I want them stopped."

"I want them stopped, too," Michael said with as

much fervor as he could. "I want to stop them from hurting more boys."

"There are always more boys," Craig intoned. His eyes lifted to Michael's for the first time since he'd entered the room. "That's what they told me when I tried to refuse, to run, when I fought them. There are always more boys to replace me with, so I better get with the program or I'll end up in a dumpster and no one will care." His voice hitched in the end, as if he choked back tears.

Brown started rise. "I think we're done for the day."

Michael ignored her and so did Craig, thankfully, sticking to his chair. "Was the man they call Boss at the house that night?" Michael pressed.

"Yes, I heard them talking about it as the guy they'd sold me to for a couple of hours yanked me out of the room." Another shudder ran through him. He still stayed sitting, and after a second, Brown reseated herself.

"Did you see him?"

"No. I'm sorry," he added. "But I remember one of the guys saying Boss was a rich dude who liked slumming it sometimes."

Michael tried to contain his excitement. This was something he hadn't heard before. "Slumming it how?"

"You know, fucking guys in those dirty places they kept us in. Like that somehow made it more fun or something." Craig made a face. "The way those places smelled, it made me want to puke, but I guess it was a turn-on for the rich dude. Or that's what I heard anyway. And he didn't do it often, I guess. One guy bragged how he'd been to Boss's real home and how it was like something you'd see on TV."

"Did this boy say where it was located?"

Craig shrugged. "No. He said they put a hood over his head, like he was a P.O.W. or something."

Hiding his disappointment, Michael reassured him. "It's okay. It's useful information." He put his book and pen away. "How are you doing?" He asked because he cared. Someone had to in addition to the earnest Ms. Brown.

The kid shrugged again. "Fine. I'm mostly staying in the infirmary. They're going to keep me there for a few more days."

"Is there a foster family lined up yet?" he asked Brown, not that it was his business necessarily. He was pretty sure he'd gotten all he could out of the boy.

Brown scrunched up her face briefly. "Not yet. There's a shortage as you know, and it's hard with teenagers."

Yeah, he did know, and it pissed him off all over again that, in addition to everything else that had happened to him, this poor kid didn't have a nice home to go to. And at fifteen, he had over two years left in the system. It sucked even though it was miles better than being in a prostitution ring. There was nothing he could do, except make sure no more kids became Craig.

Standing up, he offered his hand to the boy. "Thank you, Craig. I know talking about it with me is hard. I appreciate your help."

He stayed there with his hand out until the boy slowly stood up and gave it a quick, tense shake. It wasn't much given the long road of recovery for the boy, but it was a start.

****

"I don't like it," Ronan said between mouthfuls of food.

"You don't have to like it," Finn reminded him. "You just have to leave the house after dinner."

"Why? We're all cops here. It's not like you're having a date or anything."

Finn winced at his brother's choice of words, but said nothing. He didn't have to. Daire reached over and smacked Ronan on the arm.

"Ow! What's that for?"

"For being a dick," Daire replied with the stern glare he'd perfected after their parents died and he'd taken over as head of the family. It was eerie how his brother had managed to channel both Mom and Dad at the same time.

Finn appreciated his oldest brother's support, yet wished he'd picked another word to describe Ronan's behavior. Anything touching on the subject of Finn's unbridled libido was almost painful. Every damn night since he first met Caruso, he'd dreamt of the man. Disturbing dreams, hot ones, ending in Finn having to do an early morning load of laundry so there was no chance Daire noticed the inevitable remnants of them. Christ, it was like he was really a teenager again, endlessly fascinated with his new working toy. Even jerking off to some safe fantasy before going to sleep hadn't curbed the dreams.

Things would calm down soon, though, in that department at least. Two more days and Finn would be out in the field, trying to lure the ring into picking him up. He was both nervous and excited to get started.

"I've checked the guy out," Ronan said after a few seconds of moping. "Caruso, I mean. He's got a good rep."

"No, shit," replied Daire in a bored tone. "I checked him out, too, even after Bates assured me the guy was solid."

Finn didn't bother to be annoyed at his brothers. Their overprotectiveness was so integral to his life he only fought it when it got unbearably intrusive. "You mean despite the fact that he's gay?" Damn, where had that snarky question come from? His brothers had been nothing but supportive since he'd come out. Just another sign of his nerves he supposed.

Ronan gave him a confused look. "He's gay?"

"You didn't know that?" Finn looked at Daire who shrugged.

"I didn't tell him. It didn't seem relevant. You know, other than reassuring me he'd have your back."

Ronan shrugged, too. "It didn't come out, as it were, when I talked to people on the force who knew him. Maybe he's not out."

"Or maybe no one said anything because it's not worth mentioning." Finn really hoped that was the case, although he couldn't forget how Caruso himself said his orientation hadn't exactly been shouted from the rooftops. Well, so what? It didn't matter if Caruso was openly gay or not. They weren't in a relationship. Weren't ever going to be in a relationship. So why did that thought sour his stomach?

He stood up and gathered his dishes. "Whatever. He's due in twenty minutes. Finish up, please, and get lost." He didn't bother to wait for a response.

He was like a cat on a hot tin roof while he waited for his brothers to leave and for Caruso to arrive. It was tough, but he managed to keep his antsiness under control until he was alone in the house. The minute his brothers were out the door, however, he paced around the living room, waiting for the doorbell to ring. When it finally did, his stomach did a flip-flop.

"Get a grip, Callaghan," he mumbled to himself as he went to answer the door.

Caruso wasted no time rushing into the house so as few people as possible might see him. As usual the guy was casually irresistible in an untucked button-down shirt and worn jeans. Finn didn't have the discipline to resist checking the guy's perfect bubble butt as it walked by him. He felt a moment's guilt before shrugging it off. He was a guy, and looking was what guys did. Girls probably did it, too. Maybe he'd work up the courage one day to ask his cousin, Regan. Then again, she was almost like a third brother, so perhaps what she did wasn't the norm for her gender.

Anyway, he wasn't going to act on his desire, and that's what counted.

"Can I get you something to drink?" he asked per usual as he followed Caruso into the living room.

"No, I'm good, thanks." Caruso stood with his hands jammed inside his pockets, also per usual, looking a little awkward, which was kind of endearing. "Wash has pneumonia as it turns out." He shook his head. "I've known him for years, since the academy, and he's rarely been sick and never has taken a sick day. Now, he's down for at least a week or more." Shaking his head again, he paced around the room much as Finn had done moments earlier.

"Thing is I need a replacement. We can't go into this operation a man short." He stopped with his head bowed and peered up at Finn. "I was thinking about pulling your brother in."

"Daire?" Finn couldn't hide his surprise.

"No, he's too high up the food chain. It would attract attention. I meant Ronan."

"Oh." Finn wasn't sure how he felt about that. It would be a little like having a chaperone on a date. "He's a murder cop," was all he could think to say.

Caruso chuckled. "I know. All you Callaghans are murder cops. My lieutenant can swing a temporary transfer, and I figure he already knows what's going on. I don't want to drag anyone else into it. The fewer people who know, the better."

"Yeah, I get it. Of course, he knows. It's how we get him out of the house while you're here." With his hands on his waist, Finn rocked back on his heels and tried to think of a flaw in the plan. Ultimately, he couldn't because there wasn't one.

"Okay. I'll text him to come back." He took out his phone and sent a short message to Ronan, knowing he was with Daire and they'd both hotfoot it home. "You're making my brothers' night, you know. The idea of one of them babysitting me on the assignment will send them over the moon with joy."

Caruso's answering grin was more of a grimace. "I have three older sisters, so I hear you." He waited for Finn to send the text before adding, "Look, we've gone over everything well enough between us. The only thing left to do is decide on what you're going to wear and carry into the assignment."

"Clothes and a backpack," Finn replied with a shrug.

Caruso's chuckled. "Yeah, but what kind? Let's go up to your room and you can show me."

"Okay." Finn headed to the stairs, hiding how flustered he felt taking Caruso to his bedroom, the place where all of those inappropriate dreams had taken place. Good thing he'd been obsessive about the laundry and airing the room out. At least it didn't smell like sex. Caruso's heavy footsteps sounded behind him, and Finn couldn't help but wonder if the guy was checking out his ass.

"Have you been watching Disney's teen shows?" Caruso asked.

Finn made a face no one could see. "Yes, and I think I've lost fifty I.Q. points in the last few days."

Caruso chuckled again. "No doubt. You need to sound the right age, though, and it doesn't take more than a few years for slang and cultural references to change."

"I know. Watching those shows makes me feel old."

"Join the club." Caruso stopped next to Finn by the entrance to the bedroom. "Wait 'til you turn thirty."

There was no more than a foot between them. For a few seconds, Finn could only stare at the other cop, specifically his face. Faint lines were visible around Caruso's eyes. It gave him a look of maturity and that was definitely a turn-on.

Clearing his throat self-consciously, he said. "At least everyone knows you're an adult. It's weird to look young and feel old at the same time."

Caruso's eyes bore into him. "In this case, it's a good combo. Just what we need." His gaze dropped to Finn's lips, or at least it appeared to, and lingered there for a heartbeat, then two, before breaking away. "So, you're clothes."

"Ah, yeah. Here's what I was thinking." Finn had gone through his wardrobe and pulled out old clothes from high school which he figured should still fit. He'd also found his old school knapsack buried deep in the back of his closet. He pointed to the pile he'd placed on his desk.

Caruso walked over and picked up the T-shirt and jeans. Looking them over, he nodded. "This looks good. Thank God teenage grunge hasn't changed much in the last twenty years." He went through the rest of the stuff, including the backpack. "Works for me, except…"

"Except what?" Finn had moved away, the vision of Caruso pawing through his clothes was a little too intimate for him.

Caruso glanced over at Finn. "Are you sure these still fit? You've obviously filled out some since high school." As they had once before, Caruso's cheeks pinked up, and he averted his gaze to stare instead at some point past Finn's head.

"Um, I guess I should try them on."

"I think you should," Caruso agreed, and his face turned even redder.

He handed the clothes over to Finn and stepped over to the window. He took his phone out and played around with it, looking at email maybe, although Finn understood Caruso was really avoiding watching him change. Which was fine by Finn, except it wasn't okay with his lizard brain. That primitive and idiotic thing wanted Caruso to glance his way and see his body as he shucked down to his boxer briefs. Fortunately, the other man was far more under control. Or perhaps he wasn't interested in Finn at all.

That thought should have brought relief. Instead, it

kind of pissed him off. Finn knew he was a good-looking guy with a body he worked hard to keep fit and sculpted. He'd never had trouble attracting other guys before. Why wouldn't Caruso, the supposedly gay cop, find him hot? And, this whole line of thought was totally inappropriate and ran the risk of making it even harder to pull on his old jeans.

With a grimace, he yanked up his zipper and snapped his jeans shut. Snug. As was the T-shirt he pulled over his head. He took a few tentative deep breaths. Nothing popped or ripped open, although he couldn't say he was comfortable. He felt like a man in kids clothing, which was kind of the whole idea. The question was, would the rest of the world think so.

"What's the verdict?" he asked a still distracted Caruso.

At Finn's question, the man looked over, looked him over, and kept staring and staring and staring.

Chapter Four

The verdict? The verdict was Finn Callaghan was even hotter in the tight clothes that hugged his body like a second skin. The guy stood with arms akimbo, looking exactly how they wanted him to look—like a teenage boy. A fairly muscular one, but that was okay. The ring's clientele ran the gamut of who they were interested in fucking. Not all of them wanted skinny boys who seemed even younger than they were. Some wanted just what Finn would be offering, young yet masculine, jockish, and vulnerable in equal measure. With his face clean-shaven, his hair a little longer and clothes that were practically painted on, he would attract the right attention.

Finn was certainly attracting Michael's attention, and it made him kind of sick. Not only was it disrespectful to ogle even internally a colleague, but what did it say about him if he was turned-on? What was the difference between him and Finn's prospective clients? Okay, so he knew Finn was really an adult, fully capable of consenting to sex. That counted for something. Not that they were going to have sex or anything. Absolutely not.

Finn frowned. "No good?"

"Huh?" Oh, right he'd been staring way too long. "It's good," he hastened to reassure him.

Finn took a deep breath. "It's not very comfortable.

I was thinner in high school."

Michael barked out a laugh. "We all were. Can you stand it?"

Finn took another breath. "I guess so."

In the next instance, Michael went temporarily insane. It was the only excuse he had for walking over to Finn, reaching out and unsnapping his jeans. In that brief moment, Michael's finger brushed up against Finn's flat abs. The muscles may have been hard, but the skin was surprisingly soft. Soft and tempting. He wanted to run his palm down them and farther, past the waistband of those snug jeans and the boxer briefs outlined by the tight fabric.

Finn's stomach quivered and rippled with the touch. His breath hitched. Michael's did as well. For long seconds, they stood there, not speaking. Michael couldn't tear himself away, yet didn't dare look up into Finn's eyes. The sound of the front door opening snapped him out of his stupor. He jumped away from Finn before his brothers came up the stairs.

He coughed self-consciously and jammed his hands deep into his pockets. Damn it, all, he was hard. The last thing he needed was for Finn not to trust him to stay professional. Not to mention there wouldn't be enough left of him to identify if the older Callaghans thought he was hitting on their baby brother. Not cool.

"You, ah, probably should go commando," he advised just as said brothers entered the room.

"What are you two doing up here?" the younger of the two asked suspiciously. As well he should, given Michael's stray thoughts.

"Figuring out my clothes." Finn's gaze skittered away from his brothers as if he too felt guilty.

Michael made himself meet the stares of the other men. He hadn't met Ronan Callaghan before, although he'd gotten word the guy was asking about him. Cops were bigger gossips than anyone. The three brothers all looked alike with their black hair, fair skin, and blue eyes. No one could say they hadn't been blessed with good looks, although it was only the youngest of them that truly took Michael's breath away. The two older ones gave him the fisheye as their gazes bounced between him and Finn.

"Jesus, boyo, if you're trying to attract perverts, you're going to succeed." Ronan gave Michael a pointed look that indicated he knew where Michael's thoughts were.

Shit!

Daire wasn't so obviously hostile. "Caruso's right, you need to lose the underwear."

Finn sighed. "Fine." He trudged past everyone and out into the hallway. A door shut two seconds later.

Michael made sure not to watch him leave. He was afraid the sight of Finn's ass in those tight jeans would give him a heart attack. He decided the best thing was to go on the offensive with the brothers before either of them got it into their heads to ask embarrassing questions or make dire threats.

"I asked Finn to text you to come home, because I'm a man short." He focused on Ronan. "My lieutenant is going to ask yours if you can be temporarily reassigned to vice. My partner is down with pneumonia."

"That's not surprising," Daire remarked. "It felt like I invited Typhoid Mary into our house the other night."

Michael let himself grin. "Yeah, Wash does things in a big way."

"Why me?" Ronan asked. "Not that I'm complaining if you're proposing I help keep my brother safe."

"I need someone I can trust, and you're the right pay grade."

"Right. Okay," Ronan stated simply.

"It's fine with me, in case anyone cares," added Daire.

Before Michael could respond, Finn returned to the room sans underwear. "Is this better? It feels slightly less tight, I have to say."

Michael nearly swallowed his tongue. Or at least it clogged up his mouth so much he couldn't speak. Just as well. What would he say anyway? Without the extra layer of cloth, the guy's cock and balls were outlined in exquisite detail. He was afraid if he opened his mouth, his tongue would fall out like some cartoon wolf ogling a hot woman. Fortunately, Ronan came to his rescue.

"Christ, Jesus, I need a drink."

"Excellent idea," echoed Daire.

The two of them all but ran Finn over in their haste to leave the room. Of course, that left Michael standing there fighting with his cock's effort to make an appearance.

Crossing his arms, Finn glared at him. "Do I pass inspection or not?"

Michael swallowed hard. "Yup," he said in a raspy voice. "I'm going to, um, join your brothers in that drink."

Then he high-tailed it out of the room as if his dick were once more on fire because it kind of was.

****

Finn hunched his shoulders and made his walk through the bus station as tentative as possible. If anyone was watching, he wanted them to see teenage boy fresh off the bus from the western part of the state, alone and miserable. He and Caruso had decided to keep his cover simple and easy to maintain. Instead of having him come from some far away mid-western state, he was still a Massachusetts boy. He had to keep his Boston accent under control, but that was something he'd tried to do all of his life.

Scuffling his way down to the great room in South Station, he reminded himself he wasn't alone. Caruso was there, as was Ronan. They'd been there for at least an hour before the bus was due to arrive, keeping an eye out for anyone who looked like they were one of the boys used by the ring to approach new marks like Finn was portraying. Because Caruso knew all the new boys were strip-searched, he couldn't wear a wire. He just had to trust his brother and his boss had his back.

Ronan was a known quantity, of course. His brother would literally take a bullet for him, the same way Finn would do for either of his brothers. Caruso was still something of an unknown quantity, although Finn had spent enough time with the other guy to know he was dedicated and deliberate. He hadn't gone into this assignment half-cocked, so to speak, so Finn was confident the plan was sound. The only real concern Finn had was about the way he found himself attracted to Caruso. The previous night in his bedroom had been a study in temptation. The more time he spent with Caruso, the more he wanted him.

The really bad news was that Caruso seemed to

feel the same way. At least, his dick did. The sergeant's pants might not have been as tight as his own, but there was no missing the interest lurking within them. Crap, just thinking about it made his snug jeans even more so. With a surreptitious grab at his crotch, he tried to alleviate the crowding. No dice. Oh, well, maybe the right people would notice and make him even more of an attractive target.

When he reached the great room, he ambled over to the McDonalds stall and made a show of pulling crumpled dollar bills out of his pocket and counting them out. Then he sat at one of the tables strewn about and tore into the meager meal of hamburger, fries and a coke. Nervous as he was, the food had less appeal than they normally would. Regardless, he had a role to play, and a kid recently kicked out of his home with limited resources would be grateful to afford this much. Wolfing down the meal, he kept his head down while his eyes took in his surroundings.

Being just past the evening rush hour, there were few people around. It was easy to spot Ronan dressed up as a transit cop, making the rounds. Caruso was harder to spot. He sat on the floor over by one wall wearing an army issue jacket that looked like he'd found it in the bottom of a dumpster. With a knitted hat on his head and a few days' worth of stubble, he managed to look like the homeless man he was pretending to be. Other than a dozen or so people in suits waiting for later trains, there wasn't much going on.

He shoved the last of the food in his mouth and got up. He tossed the trash in a bin on his way to the men's room. Maybe someone was hanging out in there. A professional looking man was washing his hands, but otherwise the place was empty. Partly to dawdle and partly because he really did need to pee, he used the urinal. Another man came in while Finn washed his hands. He looked at Finn through his reflection in the mirror over the sink. For a second, Finn thought he might approach him. Although clearly not part of the ring, it might be a john who used the ring. The moment passed, however, and the guy went over to the urinal without giving any sign he was interested in more than relieving himself.

Finn left the restroom and sat down again. He'd put a paperback in his knapsack, so he took it out and pretended to read. He and Caruso had gone over what he could do to stick around a few hours at the train station. Other than eating and shopping at one of the kiosks, reading was his next best option. He kept alert for any signs of someone watching him. Time dragged on and nothing happened.

Ronan stopped on his endless loop of the great room in front of Caruso. Crouching down, he spoke to the other cop, although Finn was too far away to catch anything. A few seconds later, Ronan stood up and so did Caruso. Then Ronan walked away while Caruso made a show of picking up his own duffle bag and sneering at Ronan's back as he shuffled out of the station.

That was Finn's cue to leave as well. They'd decided to give the place a couple of hours before heading home. It wouldn't do for the real transit cops to start wondering about a boy hanging around for a long time. Picking up his pack, Finn headed out the main doors. The next play was to walk slowly toward

Chinatown and see if anyone approached him. No one did, although there were plenty of people milling about. He was almost at Tremont Street before a car slowed down.

"Hey, kid, need a ride?"

Finn stopped and walked closer to the curb. Bending down, he looked into the open window of the passenger side of a standard American-made sedan. A very different looking Caruso peered back at him. In case he was being watched, Finn hoisted his pack higher on his shoulder and glanced around him.

He stepped off the curb and clasped the door frame. "Ah, yeah, I guess so. I'm not sure where I'm going, though. I'm kind of new in town."

Caruso smiled broadly. "No problem, kid. You can hang with me for a while. Get in," he added with a toss of his head.

If anyone were watching, it was a good show of a guy picking a kid up with less than altruistic intent. Licking his lips, Finn said, "Um, okay."

He swung his backpack off and climbed into the car. Caruso raised the window as soon as Finn had the door shut and pulled back into traffic. He drove as if he were heading to the Back Bay and waited until a few blocks had passed before dropping his act completely.

"So tonight was probably a total bust, but you never know. Your brother said he saw no one hanging around who looked like they were on the prowl for the ring. I didn't see anyone, either. They could have been there anyway. I don't think anyone followed you out of the station. Again, maybe I missed them.

Finn was silent for a second. He doubted Caruso missed anything. Still, he was impatient. Even though he knew it had been a long shot that he'd be approached the first night, he'd still hoped it would happen.

"Okay, so I go back tomorrow."

"Right, in the morning. Make it seem like you managed to cage a night with some guy and are back for a cheap breakfast. Hang out for a few hours before walking over to the Common if the weather holds. Otherwise, stay there all day."

He glanced at Finn. "Don't get discouraged. This could take weeks, if it works at all."

"I know," he replied with a sigh.

"I'll take you home. Remember, it's okay to shower tonight, but don't wash your clothes. Your story has to remain that you got into town tonight, and while a trick might let you shower, he wouldn't offer you laundry services."

"Right."

Caruso chuckled. "Welcome to the glamorous world of undercover work."

They were both quiet on the relatively short ride to Charlestown. Tired as he was, Finn was also intensely aware of Caruso's closeness. In the confines of the car, the size and heat of the man was impossible to ignore. He'd ditched the grungy coat he'd been wearing in the station and wore a T-shirt and jeans. The guy had some serious muscles straining the fabric of both items of clothing. Finn couldn't help wondering what it would feel like to run his hands over those bulges, to have them wrapped around him. Looking at Caruso, he realized he'd only ever been with boys before, teenage boys and college boys his own age.

Caruso was a man. The kind of man that could pick Finn up, hold him down, fill him up as he drilled him into the mattress.

A small noise escaped Finn's lips, a sound embarrassingly like a whimper.

The car jerked slightly as Caruso shot him a look. "You okay?"

"Ah, yeah." Oh, Christ, was that even his voice? He sounded like Mickey Mouse.

Caruso shot him another look, one that clearly conveyed his skepticism. Finn switched his gaze to look out the side window while he fought to get himself under control. His dick throbbed painfully in its cramped confines. Good enough for him. Having these thoughts about his boss while on the job was wrong. The last thing he needed was Caruso dumping him from the assignment because he was acting like a horny teenager instead of a displaced one.

It was a relief when Caruso finally pulled up in front of the Callaghan house. Finn had to look at him as he fumbled with the door handle. "I'll head over to South Station first thing." His voice no longer squeaked, but it had a breathless quality and it wasn't caused by the jeans he wore cutting off his circulation.

"Sounds good. Hey," Caruso added before Finn could push the door fully open. "You did great."

As he handed out the praise, his hand landed on Finn's thigh. The warmth of the large palm seeped through the worn denim and crept up Finn's leg right to his groin. Breath exploded out of his mouth as his cock stiffened even more. Then his gaze locked on Caruso's. Caught and mesmerized, Finn stared and stared some more. The amazing thing was that Caruso stared back. In the quiet of the car, the sound of their increasingly labored breathing engulfed them.

"I feel it, too," Caruso said finally in a low voice. "The attraction. I don't want to, and I tell myself to knock it the fuck off, but…" He shook his head.

Finn fought to unscramble his brain and come up with a suitable reply. Before he could, Caruso leaned over and claimed Finn's mouth with his own. The kiss was gentle at first, almost tentative. When Finn leaned into it, the intensity shot up, Caruso's tongue pushing past Finn's lips. They played a heated game of chase for a while that bobbed back and forth between their mouths. Caruso won when he grabbed the back of Finn's head and pulled him in tight.

The hand that had rested on Finn's thigh slid to cup the straining mass of cock and balls trapped within the tight jeans. Caruso squeezed as he used the weight of his whole body to shove Finn harder against his seat. Finn's cry was swallowed up by Caruso's ravaging mouth. The intensity of the assault sent a frisson of fear up his spine, but instead of fighting to get free, Finn wrapped his arms around Caruso's broad back and pulled him in closer. Even with cloth between them, he could feel the outline of the man's muscles. It felt like power and safety. He could have stayed trapped by Caruso all night.

The kiss ended abruptly when Caruso let go of Finn all at once, his body yanking back as if pulled by strings. Then they were back to staring and panting, except now Caruso had a wild look in his eyes and Finn wasn't willing to play passive. He lunged for the other man and managed to land one kiss and cop one half-assed feel before Caruso pushed him away. He kept Finn at bay with one hand splayed across Finn's chest.

"No, sorry, we can't do this."

"Seriously?" Finn was incredulous. "Who tackled whom here anyway?"

Caruso rubbed his free hand down his face. He was puffing like a marathoner heading up heartbreak hill. "I know. Fuck, I know. It was wrong of me, okay? I apologize. If you want to file a sexual harassment complaint, I won't fight it."

With a groan, Finn threw himself back against his seat. "Don't be such a dick, Caruso."

"Michael. Once you exchange spit with someone, you have to be on a first name basis."

Finn rolled his eyes. "Michael. I'm not going to file a fucking harassment complaint against you when you only did what I wanted to do anyway."

Caruso—no, Michael—tugged at his hair with both hands. "I'm the senior officer, so it's my duty to refrain from inappropriate conduct." He paused. "Jesus, forget the department. If one of your brothers saw us, I'd be chained to a piling in the harbor waiting for the tide to come in."

"Don't worry about my brothers." Finn shook his head, a move lost on Michael given he stared anywhere except at Finn. "I'm a grown man."

"Tell them that. Besides, what does it say about me that I'm attracted to you even when you're dressed like a school boy?"

"It's not like I'm wearing knickers or anything. And even if I were, it's no different than when a woman dresses like a cheerleader to spice things up with her husband."

Michael moaned. "Not helping 'cause that's kind of skeevy, too."

Finn chuckled. "Seriously, you're such a prude."

They were quiet for a few minutes. Finn knew he should just laugh the whole thing off and leave the car. Instead, he sat quietly and ached and hoped for—he didn't know what. Michael was right that getting involved was wrong for a whole host of reasons, not the least of which was it might distract them from the assignment.

"I haven't had sex in over a year," Michael confessed in a quiet voice.

Really? Well that was—interesting. A great looking guy like Michael would have his pick of men, women, whatever. He told himself it was none of his business and asked anyway. "How come?"

Michael made a face. "It's sort of self-imposed celibacy. I feel like I'm not being honest about my sexuality, so instead of skulking around, I mostly shut it down." A few more seconds ticked by before he continued.

"Remember when I said I wasn't out with my family? Well, they're good people, but I'm only second generation American. A lot of my older relatives, like my grandparents, came from a small village. They're pretty conservative. They live in the real world and are basically decent, so they don't actively discriminate and have a live and let live mentality. They kind of shrugged about gay marriage and went about their business. There's a difference, though, between what other people do and what a family member does. I don't really know how they'd react if I came out and that scares me."

He shifted to look at Finn. "You come from a big Irish family. You must know what I mean."

Finn shifted, too, in order to face Michael more

squarely, ignoring the temptation the man's proximity created. "Yeah, I know what you mean." He dropped his gaze. "I was fourteen when my parents were killed. I was going to come out to everyone before I started high school. It seemed the right time to do it, you know?" he asked, glancing up.

Michael smiled wanly. "I get it."

"Then my world came crashing down. Daire and Ronan took up the roles of our parents, making sure my life went on as best it could. Daire was already on the force and Ronan moved back from living at Boston College to commute from home. They put their lives on hold for me, and I didn't want to add more to their plate by telling them I was gay. I knew they'd worry extra about me. They didn't need that." Placing his hand on Michael's shoulder, a gesture meant as comfort and nothing more, he said, "So, I guess we have more in common. Maybe all gay men and lesbians have that in common. Timing matters."

"But you came out eventually and I haven't, not really. Not to the people who count the most."

"Denying yourself sex isn't going to make things better. You don't need to wear a hair shirt over it."

Michael laughed. "A Catholic boy, just one more thing we share."

"True. And because we do have similar backgrounds, I have to wonder how do you fend off questions from relatives about settling down?" Finn asked in air quotes.

Michael's face clouded over. "Oh, they pretty much leave me alone on that score."

He said nothing further, and sensing that it was an even more sensitive topic, Finn let it go. Before he could think of anything more to say, a rap against his window made them both jump. Ronan peered into the car. Opening his door, Finn let his brother stick his head in.

"What are two doing hanging out like this? Someone might see you." A frown creased Ronan's face.

"Just getting our ducks lined up for tomorrow," Michael lied smoothly.

To head off any more questions, Finn pushed his way past his brother and stepped out on the sidewalk. "Later," he tossed back at Michael and headed up the stoop.

He didn't bother to watch Michael leave and raced up to his room before Ronan could pester him with any more unwanted questions.

****

The thing about moving out of his childhood home was that Michael couldn't afford to live in the city. His apartment was just north of Boston in Medford, close enough for a relatively easy commute, far enough to give him time to mentally flay himself. What a stupid asshole he was, kissing Finn Callaghan, his subordinate. A sexual harassment complaint would be the least of his problems. The Callaghan brothers both had serious reputations as asskickers. And there was a cousin, a woman he'd heard was even scarier when crossed. Thank God, Ronan had come upon them after that insane kiss.

Insane as in a profoundly crazy thing to do. Insane as in off the charts hot. His lips still sizzled from the tactile memory of Finn's mouth fused to his own. The sweet taste of Finn lingered on his tongue, which only fueled his anger at himself. But he couldn't deny how much he'd enjoyed clutching Finn's body to his, feeling the hardness of the man's cock through those tight sexy jeans. Michael's cock had been equally hard and remained so even as he put distance between himself and temptation.

He'd been fighting the attraction since the beginning and had thought he had it under control. He'd been wrong, so, so very wrong. If only the ring had taken the bait, Finn would be headed undercover, and there'd be no time to dwell on his desire for the younger cop. Instead, he'd be focused on keeping him safe and bringing "Boss" to justice.

That's not the way the night had gone, and there was nothing to be done except accept his mistake and acknowledge his weakness. Clearly, Finn couldn't be counted on to be the gatekeeper, not based on the way the guy had reciprocated the kiss. Holy fuck! Finn might be younger, but he wasn't some shy virgin. He knew what to do with what Michael was offering and had upped the ante. The ache in Michael's balls confirmed it.

His cock still raged inside his pants as Michael pulled into the driveway of the duplex he rented. It was late enough that he didn't give two thoughts to the obvious sign of his arousal. Taking the front steps two at a time, he let himself into his apartment and went straight to the refrigerator. He downed half a bottle of beer in one long swallow. Not that the cold drink did anything to ease his discomfort. He didn't even fight the impulse to jump into the shower with the bottle in hand.

The pounding spray of hot water loosened all the

kinks and strains in his body except the one that really counted. His dick jutted out and his balls stopped hugging his body only a fraction from the heat. He clasped his cock while he tipped back his head to empty his beer. Squeezing his hard flesh, he tried not to think of Finn. Yeah, that was so not going to work. He'd been trying it for the past week and had failed every time.

Why fight it? Who was going to know? Certainly not Finn. Michael wouldn't admit under torture that Finn was Michael's newest favorite fantasy. Putting the bottle aside, he soaped up his free hand and let it join the other one, slicking up his cock. He groaned loud and long. Again, who was going to know, who was going to hear?

Maybe Finn would like the idea of Michael beating off in the shower to the memory of holding Finn in his arms. The younger man didn't seem to mind the idea of hooking up with his colleague, even knowing it wasn't professional. Finn seemed far more comfortable in his gay skin than Michael was. Finn wasn't hiding like a coward behind a long ago tragedy like Michael. Michael couldn't even imagine coming out at all to his family, let alone as a teenager. It wasn't a generational issue, either. Damn it, he wasn't that much older than Finn.

Michael jerked his rod with long, slow strokes from base to tip. He flicked his thumb through the slit and gasped at the sharp pain his nail caused as it rasped against the tender skin inside. Instead of deflating his hard-on, the small bite of discomfort amped up the pleasure. He brought his other hand down to cup and squeeze his balls.

No, Finn wasn't just younger, he was braver.

Michael pictured that almost too pretty face with lips a little puffy from Michael's assault. In a different time and place, Michael would have urged that mouth down to his lap. He would have pressed it to open up to take his cock inside all that warm sweetness.

He shuddered at the thought. It would be so good, yet not good enough. Kissing Finn and letting him suck his dick would be the warm up. Fucking the guy? Now there was an idea. Sinking into even warmer, tighter heat than his mouth was what he really wanted. Squeezing his cock hard, he imagined just how good it would be. He rocked his hips into his fist with his eyes closed, picturing Finn's taut ass.

Not good enough. He couldn't fuck whom he wanted, so he might as well fuck himself. Michael released his balls and slid a finger still slick with soap into his hole. He instinctively clenched tightly around the invasion, pulling another long moan past his lips. He couldn't reach far, just teased the entrance as he picked up the speed of the hand around his dick.

"Finn," he whispered with a breathless voice. Thrusting both his hips and finger faster, he coaxed the climax out. Staccato grunts passed his lips against the backdrop of the pounding water. His body tingled from inside and out, the mounting orgasm blossoming to meet the pinpricks of water hitting his skin.

"Finn!"

He jerked as the orgasm overtook him, twitching and gasping to the point he had to yank his finger out of his ass to brace against the wall. His legs threatened to buckle. Locking his knees he tugged his cock mercilessly to wring out the last bit of cum.

Michael stood for long minutes, panting like a dog

in the sun, letting the spray wash away the remnants of his solo party. Christ, he was acting like a teenager. Maybe he was the one who should have poured himself into tight jeans and prowled the station. He needed to get himself under control. Finn was counting on him to keep him safe. If he couldn't protect Finn against his own predatory impulses, what chance did he have to fend off anyone else?

He needed to get his shit together. And he needed to do it fast. Suppressing his sexual urges had become almost second nature to him in the last few years. Meeting Finn had knocked him off his celibacy stride. He could get it back with a little effort. It should be easier to do so, because this time there was more at stake. It wasn't only a matter of making his life easier and reducing the guilt he felt from sneaking around. Now, it meant Finn's safety.

Chapter Five

Finally, thank fuck! After two days of Finn wandering around Boston, hitting the most well-known places where homeless kids tended to hang out, someone had approached him. Michael was doing his best to blend into the background of the Common. It was easy enough to do given the time of year and the number of people wandering around. Warm weather brought out the vendors and the dog walkers and the office workers desperate for fresh air. The homeless of all ages liked to lounge on the park benches and do a little panhandling. That was still Michael's cover, although he'd changed up his clothing each day in case someone was watching Finn and noticed him too.

Ronan had proved to be aces at undercover work. He managed to put on a different uniform to blend into each location. Where he was getting this from, mystified Michael. Neither he nor his lieutenant had requisitioned anything. Ronan insisted he had it covered, and the man hadn't lied. He was outdoing himself this time, posing as a mounted cop, sitting straight on the saddle while allowing a couple of giggly young women to pat his horse's nose. Seriously, a horse? The day before he'd been on a bicycle.

None of that could be a distraction now, however. Sitting on a bench next to Finn was a mocha-skinned boy. He looked like any other urban-based teenage boy and was chatting Finn up with a cheery look on his face. Finn played it cool, leaning away from the other boy and his whole body language screaming "back off."

Good, that's exactly how they'd agreed he'd act. He was a scared kid who'd been kicked out of his home and spent the last couple of days using up his meager savings trying to survive in a city he barely knew. He'd already been picked up by a man and forced to give him head just to have a place to sleep his first night. What trust he had was all used up.

Springing up from the bench, the other boy made a gesture, as if to tell Finn to sit tight. He then ran over to a hot dog vendor and came back with a dog and a bottle of water. He offered both to Finn, who stared for a few seconds before grabbing the food. The way Finn wolfed the dog down, Michael truly believed he was starving. The other kid obviously did, too. He sat back down and grinned as he watched Finn. After he'd shoved the last of the food into his mouth, Finn took the water and downed most of it in a single shot. He wiped his lips with the back of his hand and looked off in the distance.

Damn, he was good. If Michael hadn't known better, he would have easily bought the story Finn was telling with his actions. The other boy put his hand on Finn's shoulder and bent his head to engage Finn in conversation. Slowly, Finn started to respond. Ten minutes later, Finn nodded and the two of them got to their feet. Michael's heart sped up. This was it. He watched them walk away, gave them a good head start, then followed.

Because they couldn't send Finn in with a wire, he and Ronan had to follow Finn. Otherwise, they'd have to wait until Finn had a chance to contact them. That wasn't acceptable. Neither he nor the Callaghan brothers were willing to let Finn go in without surveillance.

"Keep on him, Caruso," Ronan ordered into his ear. They at least could be connected. Underneath the ratty knitted hat Michael wore, there was a Bluetooth shoved into his ear. He gritted his teeth against Ronan's dictatorial tone, understanding hierarchy meant damn little when your brother was at risk. Instead, he gave a brief nod. "I'm going to pass the horse back to its actual rider and change into civvies. I'll circle around so I can pull in behind them on foot."

Again, Michael nodded. While a homeless guy could get away with talking to himself, he didn't want to take any chances of calling attention. He wasn't surprised when the two boys headed down into a T station. The ring used flophouses and seedy hotels to do their business. A new boy would definitely be tucked away in one of the houses until the ring believed it had him under control.

"They're getting on the Red Line," he murmured.

"Shit, okay, stay on them and give me a direction when you can. I'll get my car," Ronan replied.

As he headed toward the same subway entrance, Michael took the chance no one was watching him and pulled off his greasy coat. Underneath, he wore a simple long-sleeved shirt and jeans. He wadded the coat into a ball and tossed it into a trash barrel he passed without slowing down. Then he unzipped the duffel bag he carried, pulled out a messenger style briefcase, and shoved the duffel into the next barrel he saw. By the time he bolted down into the bowels of public transportation, he looked more like an office drone.

He tamped down his impatience to catch up as he shoved bills into the automated ticket machine for a one-ride Charlie ticket. Because Finn and the other boy were already out of sight, he had to take a gamble and assume they were heading outbound. Luck was with him when a train pulled in just as he arrived on the platform and he caught a glimpse of the boys entering one of the cars. He raced down to hop into the same car at the opposite end and did his best to blend into the crowd. He didn't dare do more than glance down at where the boys had found a couple of seats side-by-side. He could only see the back of their heads, which was perfect. It meant Finn's new companion wouldn't be able to see Michael during the ride.

Grabbing a strap, he braced his legs and held on tight as the train lurched out of the station.

****

"You'll like this place, straight up, man. Rizzo, the guy whose place it is, he's cool, man. He lets you hang while you get your shit together. There's always some serious grindage. You don't have to worry about going hungry. And there's places to sleep in his crib. No more park benches and underpasses, you know?"

Finn let the guy, Elvis he'd said his name was, chatter on about the awesome place he had for Finn to hang out in. He let a little of his excitement show, hoping it looked more like nervous hope that he'd found a safe place to flop. He'd done as he and Michael had agreed and played hard to get when Elvis had approached him in the park. It wasn't difficult to pretend he didn't trust this person swooping in out of the blue and trying to befriend him. The simple fact was he didn't trust Elvis. Behind the easy smile was a sharpness to the boy's eyes, a calculation, as if Finn were merchandize to evaluate.

Of course, Elvis had probably been one of the ring's victims a few years ago. He couldn't be much older than Finn's real age. Now, however, the guy was clearly on the prowl to bring in fresh meat. When Michael rained hellfire down on the ring, it would be up to someone else to decide where Elvis lay on the culpability scale. As far as Finn was concerned, he had to push down any concern that Elvis was only another victim. He had to be played as a mark in the sting operation. So Finn let him babble on while Finn kept his shoulders hunched and his gaze down.

"Hey," Elvis said, putting his arm around Finn's shoulders. "Relax, man. Everything's going to be fine, more than."

Sure, as long as Finn was willing to prostitute himself. He cringed inwardly when he thought of all the boys who'd been in the place he was pretending to be, desperate for help and willing to believe all that great food and a safe place to sleep was because this Rizzo character was a great humanitarian or just a really cool guy, as Elvis was portraying him. He didn't have to play it as a completely credulous boy, though.

He allowed his body to relax a fraction before saying, "I don't know. It sounds good, but why would he want to let me stay? I can't pay him or anything. I can't even get a job. I don't have any ID."

Elvis squeezed his arm then let him go. "I told you, man. You don't have to worry about that. Not yet, anyway. Rizzo knows people. He can help you find work if you want, even without the ID."

Finn shot him a skeptical look. "Yeah? What kind

of work."

Elvis shrugged and gave him a crooked smile. "All kinds of work out there. Something you like, you'll see. It's going to be fine."

That seemed like the guy's mantra. Elvis was slick but not necessarily bright. Finn let the topic go. It wouldn't do to press too hard at this stage. He doubted the ring was going to drop him into the deep end, as it were, right off the bat. They'd lure him in by giving him a sense of security before they'd start pressuring him into pulling his own weight. There was nothing to do now except let Elvis lead him to their destination and hope Michael and Ronan were on their tail.

Speaking of which, he looked at the window across the aisle as the train swayed its way down the dark tunnel of the underground system. He saw a reflection that goosed his courage. Michael had succeeded in sticking with them enough to be in the same car. He looked nothing like he had on the Common. God, the man was good at undercover work. Finn had no doubt Michael would change his appearance again once they left the train. He shifted his stare to a point straight ahead so Elvis wouldn't try to follow his gaze. Chances were he wouldn't recognize Michael as one of the homeless men from the Common, but he didn't want to risk it.

It helped, though, to have Michael nearby. It gave Finn a sense of safety. He'd known the man for less than two weeks, and yet he trusted him already with his life. And with each passing day, he felt more intimately connected than they actually were, his desire for Michael growing. It was the damn dreams, every fucking night. He hadn't soiled so much of his underwear in years, and it was embarrassing even though no one knew about it except himself. He wondered if Michael was having a similar problem. Ever since that first night undercover and the mutual attack in the car, he at least knew the attraction, if not obsession, wasn't one sided.

I feel it, too.

He flushed with heat at the memory. His heart had skipped a beat at hearing those words, and he'd become even harder than he'd already been as soon as Michael grabbed him for a kiss. If Michael hadn't put on the brakes, Finn would have gladly straddled the guy's lap and ground them both to climax. The older, cooler head had prevailed. Or maybe the more cowardly one had. Michael was the more mature and experienced of them, but he was also a bit fucked up about his sexuality.

Half in the closet and half out, and Jesus, no sex in a year? That should be more of a turn-off than it was. The sad truth was Finn still wanted to jump the guy and ride his dick into oblivion.

"This is our stop," Elvis said, tossing Finn out of his reverie.

Finn glanced up at the sign for the stop and confirmed they were getting out where they suspected the ring kept some of their safehouses. He forced himself not to look in Michael's direction as he allowed Elvis to take him by the arm and lead him from the train car.

Once on the street, Elvis kept a rapid pace, taking Finn down a series of side streets and alleys. Apartment buildings and houses lined their way, some well-maintained, others not so much. There were people everywhere going about their business. But the street corners contained small groups of boys and young men, some of whom made kissing noises and catcalls as Elvis hustled Finn past.

"Don't let those assholes bother you. Once you're under Rizzo's protection, no one will dare bother you around here."

They entered a small street that contained more rundown tenement style housing. Elvis peeled off up the cracked front walk of a two story house at the end of the street that looked out of place given its location. It was nice-looking, almost homey, as if a family lived there with a little more time, money, and the inclination than most had in the neighborhood to keep it up. It was not what Finn had been expecting, and that was probably the intent. It didn't look like a place where bad things happened.

Elvis whistled tunelessly as he raced up the front steps. The front door opened before he got to it, and another boy stepped aside as Elvis shoved through with Finn in tow.

The dark-skinned boy gave Finn the once-over. "Who's the new boy," the kid asked in the lilt of a Caribbean accent.

"None of your business," Elvis replied cheerfully without a hitch to his step. "Come on, Finn. Rizzo'll want to meet you, then we can find you a place to sleep."

Finn took in his surroundings with a brief once over. The rooms on either side of the narrow hallway they went down were furnished fairly decently, albeit cheaply. He caught a glimpse of a large flat screen to his right, and a bunch of boys were hanging around watching it. That was all he could see before Elvis propelled him into a large kitchen.

A shirtless man with a shaved head, bulging muscles, and enough tats to obscure most of his arms and chest sat at a beat-up wooden table. A redheaded boy sat on his lap. The kid wore nothing more than blue briefs, and with a sickening feeling, Finn realized this boy couldn't be any older than thirteen. Michael had warned him some of the boys were going to be very young and Finn had to resist the temptation to just bust the men he could find. They needed to get to the top or this ring would continue.

The man jiggled his leg, bouncing the boy. Dangling him on his lap the way Finn remembered his grandfather and Uncle Finnegan doing. Except there wasn't anything innocent about the way the man's arms encircled the boy's thin waist. The boy had his arms around the man's neck, and in the brief moment he bothered to look Finn in the eye, Finn saw wariness and a bit of fear. Finn shoved aside his mounting anger and made himself mimic the expression as he looked at the man.

"Who do we have here, Elvis?"

"This is Finn, Rizzo. I met him hanging out on the Common. He's got nowhere to stay."

"That so?" Rizzo gave Finn a friendly smile, although it was easy to see through the surface of it. The calculation and avarice lurking in those eyes made Elvis look like a saint in comparison. This man really was seeing the dollars and cents residing in Finn's body.

He swallowed hard, again making one emotion seem like another, more vulnerable one. "Yes, sir."

Rizzo boomed out a laugh and squeezed the

redhead closer to him. "Well, aren't you the polite one. Where're you from?"

"Out by Springfield."

"Yeah? What you doing coming to Boston on your own?"

"His folks kicked him out, Rizzo," Elvis interjected.

Rizzo shot him a hard look. "I was asking Finn." Elvis nodded and took a step back. Rizzo's smile returned. "Irish, huh?"

"Yes, sir."

"Why'd your folks kick you out, Irish?"

Biting his lip, Finn hunched his shoulders and looked at the ground. "They found out I was gay." He made his expression defiant as he looked up again. "I don't care. I don't need them. I'm fine the way I am."

Rizzo's leg jiggled some more. "Hmm, yes, you are. Very fine." The smile he gave Finn was less inviting and more predatory. "Well, you don't have to worry about that with us." Giving another squeeze to the boy, he said, "As you can see, we're very gay friendly around here."

That statement, equating being gay with being a pedophile, ramped up Finn's pissed factor to an eleven. Still, he swallowed down his bile and played his part.

Glancing at Elvis, he said, "Yeah, that's what Elvis said. It's nice. Kind of weird, honestly, but nice."

Rizzo laughed again. "I like you, Irish. Elvis, find our friend here a bed." He treated Finn to a megawatt smile. "You're welcome here, Finn. This is a safe place for you."

Sure, so long as he didn't mind being abused. "Thank you, sir."

"Rizzo's fine."

"Rizzo."

Elvis grabbed Finn's arm. "Come on."

Finn allowed Elvis to turn him around before digging in his heals and looking at Rizzo over his shoulder. "I don't have any way of repaying you, Rizzo."

"You let me worry about that, Irish. Go on."

This time, he let Elvis tug him out of the room.

****

Michael jumped into the beater before Ronan had brought it to a complete stop. He took a second to admire once more the Callaghan brother's ability to conjure up the right vehicle at the right time. The older model car, held together with rust and various tones of paint, looked right at home in this neighborhood. As did the man himself, having ditched his mounted cop uniform for a T-shirt, jeans, and a gimme with a trucking logo on it. As proud as Michael was with his own quick-change outfits, Ronan was giving him a run for his money. He'd bet, too, that Ronan hadn't been forced to ditch stuff the way Michael had on the fly. The shirt he'd ripped off as he left the T stop had been a present from his mother. Not a favorite or anything, but still. And the messenger bag that resided in the same trash can as the shirt had cost him enough to make him wince at the loss.

None of which mattered a damn now that Finn was right where they wanted him to be. Michael knew he should be elated his plan had worked. On some level, the cop one, he was. The man part of him who had tasted Finn and craved more was beating back a sense of terror. Finn was trapped inside a very bad place, and

Michael's gut already had holes in it from the worry chomping away.

"We need to get eyes and ears on that house ASAP."

"You're preaching to the choir, Caruso," Ronan snapped as he spun the wheel to take a corner faster than he should. "How quickly can you get your tech guys out here and how do you intend to set up surveillance without being obvious about it in this neighborhood?"

Michael punched numbers into his phone, the plan mostly formed in his head. He'd known there was a chance of Finn being taken to a more residential part of Boston. Now that he had an address, if they could find a rental property, they could set up shop without a hassle. He hoped. He needed more help, though. His call was answered on the third ring.

"What's up, man?" The voice on the other end sounded better than it had the last time they'd spoken.

"Wash, the possibility we spoke of has become a reality. I hope you're up for convalescing somewhere other than home."

"I've been praying to the little baby Jesus that you'd call." Wash's voice dropped low. "Jeanie is driving me batshit crazy with her nursing efforts. I need out in a major way."

Michael chuckled. "Good to hear, but you have to run interference with her. I don't want to be knocked flat by your wife when I come to pick you up."

"No problem, man. She and the kids are going to a school event in about two hours. Pick me up then, and I'll leave a note."

"Coward," Michael said even though he applauded

the move.

"You know it."

"Pack a bag. I'll be there in two and give you the run down. Bottom line is, our boy, Finn, is in."

Hanging up with Wash, Michael's next call was to one of the two surveillance guys he'd tapped. It didn't take long for them to confirm there were exactly zero rentals on the street. Michael swore violently as he hung up. Ronan frowned at him.

"Did you really think they'd take him to some warehouse district with lots of vacant buildings?"

"I was hoping, yeah," Michael retorted. Shit, there were always places to rent in Boston. Just their luck for Finn to be kept on a fully occupied street. If they tried to use a van, it would catch people's attention. They had to find a way to get into one of the homes or apartments near the house.

"Turn around and go back," he said to Ronan. The other cop did as told without more than a raised eyebrow. "Come at it from the back of the house."

When Ronan swung down the street that ran parallel to one where Finn was being held, Michael kept his eyes open for something that might do the trick. He broke into a wide grin when his wishes were granted. One of the houses on the street was boarded up, the remnants of a fire still visible on parts in the form of black streaks. The place wasn't empty, however. He could see people lounging on the steps and suspected it was being used as a drug house by locals. Well, that was easily rectified.

"Okay, let's head to the station," he ordered Ronan as he punched numbers into his phone once more.

****

They could hear the smack of flesh against flesh and the cry of pain, the pleading of a boy, the angry voice of a man. Michael gripped his coffee with white knuckles and was glad he held a plastic refillable mug instead of a paper cup. God, he only thought he'd hated the man they called Rizzo. Now, he knew he loathed him and wanted more than anything to crash into that seventh circle of hell and get Finn and all the boys being exploited out of there. It physically hurt to stand there and just listen day after day and not be able to do anything.

Wash shuffled over to him. The poor guy was far from well, but he did look happy being out of the house. It hadn't taken much to send cops over to roust out the drugged-out floppers. While the event had attracted attention from the neighbors, one of them, an older woman, had conveniently covered for them by loudly proclaiming it was about time someone took her complaints about the drug house seriously. With a chorus of "yes, ma'am, thank you, ma'am" the cops had dragged all of the inhabitants out. Michael, Wash, and their two man crew had quietly set up shop in the middle of the night.

"You should take off tonight, go home, take a shower, and get some sleep," Wash advised.

The house was in sounder shape than they'd expected and they'd set up cots for napping. Bureaucracy had managed to cause the water to remain on, so they had pretty much what they needed. The vermin hadn't had time to set up house too much, either. Still, in just a few days, the place had something of survivors-of-a-plane-crash-in-the-Andes kind of feel about it. Michael didn't care. He wasn't leaving.

Shaking his head, he said, "I can't. They've had him with them long enough. Tonight may be the night they send him out to earn his keep. They've already been hinting at it."

Wash sighed. "Yeah, I know, and that Rizzo character is not exactly the patient type."

It was hard to pick up much from the house given the distance and the ambient noise of the neighborhood. They'd heard enough to know that while Rizzo was all smarmy charm with Finn, he turned on a dime with his existing stable of boys for the flimsiest of reasons. Like he was doing now. Michael sincerely hoped he'd be the one to personally put the cuffs on the bastard.

"I'm staying," Michael said and swallowed down his anxiety over Finn's safety.

****

"Stay out of it, man. It's none of our business."

Finn grimaced at Elvis. "He hit him!"

The other boy blocked Finn's view of the living room and used his body to herd Finn in the opposite direction. As much as Finn wanted to shove him back, march up to Rizzo, and break his nose, he didn't. The operation was more important than saving one boy from getting a black eye. But man it cost him.

It hadn't taken long for Rizzo's true colors to show through. He was like any pimp, nice and encouraging when his boys were bringing in the money and doing what he said. One wrong move or one low scoring night, and the fists came out.

"I'm not so sure it was a good idea for me to come here," he said as he went back upstairs. He needed to keep up the pretense of being a vulnerable runaway even though he was anxious to get turned out for the ring. He stood no chance of meeting the head guy until he demonstrated he could play their game.

"Now, why do you want to say that, man?" Elvis whined. "You've had it good here, haven't you? Food, a soft bed, no cops hassling you. And I've got something for you."

"Oh, yeah?" Finn gave him a skeptical look. "What?"

Elvis smiled mischievously. "Come and see."

Finn followed Elvis into the small back bedroom Elvis had all to himself. Besides Rizzo, he was the only one to have privacy. Finn and the other boys shared army cots in various bedrooms and rooms serving as such. There was a plastic bag sitting on the bed and Elvis dumped its contents out. Finn saw a small jumble of clothes and a pair of black running shoes.

Elvis picked up a sleeveless, shiny blue shirt and a pair of black skinny jeans with prefabbed rips. He held them out to Finn. "These are for you. And the kicks. Cost bank, I don't mind telling you." Pressing them to Finn, he said, "Go ahead and try them on."

"Um, okay."

Finn put the clothes back down on the bed, and toeing off his own sneakers, he shucked his jeans, then his shirt. Having gone commando, he was a little embarrassed to be completely naked in front of another guy in a bedroom given they weren't intending to have sex. When he reached quickly for the new stuff, however, Elvis stayed his hand.

"I know you like to free-ball it, but," he admonished with a twitch of his lips. "Try these."

Finn didn't have to fake his incredulity when presented with the blue thong. "I can't wear that."

"Sure you can," Elvis replied, pushing the scrap of cloth into Finn's chest. "It'll show off that fine ass of yours. Do it for me," he urged when Finn still hesitated.

With reluctance, part genuine and part fake, Finn took the underwear and pulled it on. He could barely contain the urge to pluck the string from between his ass, then realized he shouldn't bother to hide his discomfort.

"This feels weird," he complained as he pulled and released the thong.

"You'll get used to it," was all Elvis said. His expression held a hardness that brooked no dissent.

In silence, Finn put the rest of the stuff on. The jeans were tight enough to make him long for the relative comfort of his old clothes. The tight muscle shirt didn't even meet his waist. About a two inch strip of his bare abdomen showed. He felt like the whore he was intended to be and tried not to squirm under Elvis' scrutiny.

The guy smiled. "You look hot! Come over here so I can do something with your hair."

"What?" Finn demanded, but he didn't fight it when Elvis hauled him over to a table of product. A few seconds later, and Elvis had spiked up Finn's hair with some gel.

"Perfect. Let's go show Rizzo."

"Why?"

Elvis ignored him and, grabbing one of Finn's arms, dragged him back downstairs and into the kitchen. It was Rizzo's favorite part of the house. He sat at the table, nursing a beer. The boy he'd hit stood off to the side with a bag of frozen peas against his cheek.

Finn tried not to look at the kid, afraid his anger

would show too much in front of Rizzo. The man whistled appreciatively as his gaze raked up and down Finn's body.

"Damn, Irish, don't you dress up pretty!"

"Like him, Rizzo?" The pleading tone in Elvis' voice reminded Finn that Elvis was as trapped as any boy in the house.

Rizzo licked his lips. "Delicious." He jerked his head at the boy with the peas, his meaning clear. The kid fled the room. "I think it's time to reintroduce you to the world, Irish."

"Um, I don't understand what you mean." He kept his voice meek and uncertain while his heart beat a rapid tattoo of excitement. Finally, things were moving again.

Rizzo took a long pull of his beer. "Well, now, see. I'm not some lucky lottery winner or anything. I don't have a big pile of money I can lavish on lost boys like yourself."

Finn made a point of swallowing hard. "I know, sir. And I'm really grateful. I want to pay you back. I just don't know what kind of job I can get."

"Oh, I have the perfect job for you, Irish. You're going to love it 'cause it's easy work and it makes you feel good at the same time."

Licking his lips, Finn glanced at Elvis. The boy was nodding in encouragement or agreement. "What kind of work? I can't imagine liking any of it, but I know I have to pull my own weight."

"You'll like this, I guarantee." Rizzo winked. "You like to fuck, don't you?" He watched Finn from over the rim of his bottle as he took another slug. "Elvis tells me you popped your cherry already."

Finn dropped his gaze and wondered how he might conjure up a blush. Then he remembered that Michael and Ronan were probably listening in on the conversation. That did it.

"Yes, sir," he confirmed with a frown directed at Elvis. "I don't get how that helps with working, though."

"You strike me as a bright boy. I bet if you give it a moment's thought, you'll get what I mean."

Wiping his palms on the front of his legs in nervousness, Finn counted silently to twenty. He widened his eyes. "You want me to fuck guys for money?"

Rizzo winked again. "Knew you were smart, Irish."

"But—"

"No buts." The smile on Rizzo's face vanished. "I'm not asking you to do anything you wouldn't do like the horny twink you are. You're just going to make bank on it at the same time. It's easy. Any boy here will tell you that."

Elvis nodded his head frantically, as if pleading with Finn to agree.

Finn gave it several more seconds of thought. "I guess, but how do I find these guys?"

"You just leave that to us. Right, Elvis?" Rizzo drained his bottle and slammed it down on the table. "You be a good boy, Irish, and I'll take good care of you in return."

Finn pulled up a smile and hoped it didn't look fake. Then he thought of shoving Rizzo on his stomach and tying his wrists behind his back, and his smile became real.

Chapter Six

Finn followed Elvis out into the warm evening. It was barely sunset and already people were out socializing after dinner, or maybe they'd never even gone inside. He'd barely choked down the sandwich Elvis made for him, his stomach jittery with both nerves and anticipation. This was the tricky part. There was no way he'd be trusted enough to meet Boss unless he did a few nights of tricks first.

Michael had promised him they'd try to make sure he didn't have to go through with actually having sex with anyone, although he'd been vague on exactly how he'd keep that promise. Bottom line was, Finn was prepared to do whatever he had to. Now that he'd seen for himself the boys at risk and the life they were being forced to live, he was more determined than ever to bring this ring down.

He hefted his backpack more securely on his shoulder. All it held was what Elvis had given him for the night—condoms, lube, mouthwash, and a bottle of water. His trick bag, the boy had called it. Funny how the very things he carried while out bar hopping in college took on a sordid aspect when being used to prostitute himself. The only difference was the money, and that was plenty difference enough. Couple it with the fact that Elvis and Rizzo and everyone else involved with this ring thought he was a fifteen year old boy, and it became stomach-turning.

"Where're we headed?" he asked as they walked in the direction of the subway.

"Don't worry. There's a place we can go where men who like pretty boys hang out."

"You mean like a street corner?"

Elvis giggled. "Pretty much. It's near a nightclub."

"So, what? Am I supposed to let them fuck me in an alley?" Finn knew the answer to his question already. Michael had told him that according to the boys they rescued, the ring used seedy hotels for a lot of their business.

"Naw, nothing like that." Elvis swung his arm around Finn's shoulders and kept it there as they walked. On the surface, it felt like a comforting gesture. It also held him to the other boy's side. If Finn had been inclined to run, he'd have to fight Elvis off.

"Don't worry about a thing, man. We've got you covered. I'll show you a place to take him before we get to the club. Once a guy makes it clear he's interested in partying with you, you lead him there. Easy, private, and comfortable."

Finn stayed quiet for a while, his eyes scanning his surroundings constantly as undetectably as possible. His step hitched a millisecond when he spotted a familiar figure. Michael's partner, Washington, ambled in the same direction as they did on the sidewalk across the street. Where had he come from? Didn't matter. Obviously, Michael and Ronan had found a base of operations in the neighborhood, although why the pneumonia plagued cop was with them was a mystery. Except dressed as he was in ratty clothes, wiping his nose on his sleeve, he fit in with many of the other guys hanging around. He looked, Finn realized, like a druggie more than a sick man. And that was the point, wasn't it? Michael was fucking brilliant.

Finn didn't bother asking Elvis any more questions, just let him ramble on as they entered the T stop, rode the train to the Leather District, and joined the night crowd. "That's it over there," the guy said, pausing a moment to let Finn get his bearings.

Finn looked the place over and figured his father would have called it a hot-sheets hotel. The desk clerk no doubt was on the ring's payroll. "Okay, but, um…" He stuttered to a halt.

Elvis sighed. "What you worried about?"

Finn shrugged and stared at his sneakers. "What if the guy gets nasty, mean, you know?"

"Oh." Once again, Elvis grabbed his shoulders and hugged him as he started walking again. "Don't worry. The clerk there knows to put you in a special room. It's one we use for all of the new boys their first time. We've got eyes on that room. If the guy tries anything funny, we'll come in and take care of him."

"Really? Okay, that's good to know."

God damn, they had surveillance of their own, and of course, they'd use it to tape his first trick. It had nothing to do with keeping him safe, of course. It was insurance. If he tried to balk afterward, they'd show him the tape and threaten to mail it to the police or his parents or just put the thing up on YouTube. Clever, and it meant he'd have to go through with whatever the john wanted to do or his cover would be blown. Fucking fantastic.

****

Michael spotted Finn easily. The guy was leaning

against the wall with his fingers shoved into as much of the pockets of his skinny jeans as the fabric would allow. And he'd thought Finn's old Levis had been tight. Christ! One leg was bent and pressed against the wall which served to thrust his hips a little forward, showing off his package. At this distance, all he could see was a sizable bulge. Closer, he'd no doubt see the outline of Finn's cock and balls. As that fucker, Rizzo had said, he looked delicious.

He wiped his palms on his thighs. There had never been a time when he'd been as nervous as he was now. Not only was Finn's life on the line if he made a wrong move, but he was about to head into a hotel room with him. Sure, they weren't going to do anything, this was all about pretending. The idea still caused him to break out into a sweat. Thank God, though, Wash had been able to be their front man. Having him hang out on the front stoop to lay claim to the abandoned house had made the whole surveillance possible. Even the neighborhood watch lady had believed he was the new druggie in residence, berating him in a voice loud enough to carry over to Rizzo's house. He'd managed to track them to the T stop and stay on their tail.

Michael had barely had time to do a quick change in the car while Ronan whisked him to this part of the city. He wished he'd had more time to freshen up. He felt grubby as hell. Of course, it didn't matter. He had money, and that was all Finn's handler would care about it. It wasn't as if he were picking Finn up for a date or anything. The thin boy who was pressing Finn into prostitution, probably to keep his own skin from being flayed, lounged close to Finn. His eyes darted around, checking people out. When his gaze landed on him, Michael made sure to stay fixed on Finn.

As he approached, he plastered what he hoped was a smarmy smile on his face. "Hi, there," he said to Finn. The other boy, Elvis he'd heard him called, straightened up.

Finn's gaze flew up, and he stared back at Michael wide-eyed. It was a good act, nervous and shy, except he wasn't so sure it was an act. Finn licked his lips and took one deep breath.

"H-hi," he stuttered back as he straightened away from the wall.

"You looking for a date, man?" Elvis asked.

"Um, sorry, is he with you?" Michael asked.

"Yeah, in a way. I'm his social secretary, if you catch my drift." Elvis grinned at him.

"Oh, ah, sure. I'm looking for a date. Are you free?" Michael turned his attention back to Finn, who looked at Elvis.

Before Finn could respond, Elvis butted in again, "That depends. Are you a cop?"

Michael let his expression show surprise. "No, no way." He could lie in this situation because he wasn't trying to entrap Finn or Elvis for solicitation.

"Good, that's good."

Even though Elvis was doing all the talking, Michael kept his gaze on Finn, trying to pretend it was merely lust, when in reality, he couldn't get enough of him. Even with the surveillance, he'd been worried sick about Finn for the last few days. He needed to see for himself that the guy was okay. Finn's expression was guarded, and given the role he was playing, it made sense. Deep within his eyes, however, there was a message.

"I'm fine" seemed to be what he was trying to say. Then again, maybe that's only what Michael wanted to see.

"I can see you're really into my friend here," Elvis kept jabbering on.

"He's gorgeous." Because it was the truth, the words were easy to say. But this was like playacting, and he needed to move things along. "How much?"

"Depends on what kind of date you want."

"I want the best kind. I want to have the most fun a guy can have with a boy." Jesus, what a lame way to say he wanted to fuck Finn. He needed to act like a married suburban guy out trolling for what he shouldn't want. To emphasize his identity, he made a show of twirling the fake wedding band he'd shoved on his finger.

Elvis's gaze dropped to Michael's hand as he named a price. It was steep. Of course, it was. Child exploitation was as taboo as it got with a high price to pay if you got caught and rightly so. Michael blew out a breath.

"Wow, um, okay. I've got that on me." He reached for his wallet in his back pocket slowly, giving Elvis a chance to stop him.

"Not now, man. You pay my friend when you're done to show him how much you appreciate what he does for you."

Michael grimaced. "Right." Stepping closer to Finn, he cupped his chin with his hand. "What's your name, sweetheart?"

Finn's eyelashes fluttered a few times. "I'm Finn. Daddy."

Michael didn't have to fake a response. He

breathed out harshly as Finn's whispery tone and submissive posturing set blood racing to Michael's cock. Who knew his tastes ran to adorable twinks in muscle shirts? Maybe that's why putting his sexuality on hold had been so easy. He'd been chasing after the wrong type of men. Not that this was the time or place to psychoanalyze himself. Sliding his hand down Finn's arm, he linked their fingers.

"Do you have a place we can go?"

Finn nodded once. "This way."

He tugged Michael toward the nearest intersection, giving Elvis a quick look over his shoulder. Good, he knew just how to play it, nervous yet determined. Finn had been the perfect fit for the undercover work. A little too perfect as far as Michael was concerned. The feel of their palms pressed together made Michael's heart race. Their bodies bumped every few steps and Finn's hip rubbed against Michael's thigh. His cock rose more, straining his pants, not understanding this was all supposed to be an act.

They crossed the street with a stream of nighttime partiers. "Are we going to that hotel over there?" he asked with a jerk of his head.

"That's right. It's a nice place, Daddy. Private." Finn was keeping up the pretense as Michael had warned him to do, just in case they were in earshot of anyone in the ring. Elvis was undoubtedly watching them still.

Before they went inside the building that had seen better days, Finn pulled up short and turned to press up against Michael. No way the guy could miss the bulge in Michael's shorts, and although Finn's eyes went wide for a second, he didn't move away.

"Just a friendly warning, Daddy. My friend keeps an eye out for me. He'll know if you do anything I don't let you do."

There was a warning there. It took Michael a few seconds of staring into Finn's bright blue and very earnest eyes before he got the message.

"I understand." Bending down, he brushed a kiss on Finn's lips. "Are you fucking kidding me?" he said under his breath.

Finn gave him a slight shrug before leading him into the hotel. The clerk at the desk looked as old and as seedy as the building. He tossed an old-fashioned key on the counter when Finn mentioned Elvis's name and went back to reading his magazine. The room was on the second floor and by Michael's estimation right above where the office behind the front desk would be. That made surveillance easy, he imagined.

Finn tugged his hand free as he shut the door. Michael reluctantly let him go and did a quick scan of the room. Shabby and not very clean looking. There were probably bed bugs, but that was the least of his problems. They were being watched or at least recorded in order to be watched later. He couldn't just pretend to be Finn's john, he had to actually become it.

Holy Mother of God, he had to fuck Finn Callaghan or the whole operation would blow up in their faces. Even if he chickened out, then what? Elvis would put Finn's ass right back against that wall until a real creep stopped and asked how much. At least, he really cared about Finn, wanted him for who he was, not who he pretended to be. More importantly, Finn wanted him, too. Their mad groping in the car had proved that much.

Finn was standing by the bed, his backpack tossed on the floor, looking at Michael and waiting for him to make the first move. He had to do it. A boy with his first trick wasn't going to be the aggressor.

Because he was supposed to be nervous as well, he didn't just dive in and grab the guy. He liked to think, in those off moments when he pursued other men, he had some smooth moves. So he slowly approached Finn, keeping his eyes on him, a small smile playing across his lips. He tried not to think about how he was being at least observed if not taped and how if they were being taped, some cops would likely see it after the bust went down.

"I'm not going to hurt you," he murmured for show and because he really wanted Finn to know he would be careful with him. Even though Finn wasn't a virgin or anything, it was the first time for them. If he could just put everything out of his mind and concentrate on making this good for Finn.

Finn swallowed audibly. "I know."

There was no "daddy" tacked on, that's how Michael was sure Finn was talking to him, the real him. Good, they were on the same page with this. It was only the two of them, no one else. And yet, the setting and the circumstances of their coming together made it less awkward somehow. At this moment, it was all right to think of himself as someone else. He didn't have a big, traditional family that might not accept him for who he was. He didn't have a past weighing him down and coloring his decision to keep his sexuality on a low-flamed backburner.

He was a guy about to have sex with another guy, and God, but Finn took his breath away. It was okay to think it and to say it.

"You make my knees weak," he confessed as he closed the distance between them. Finn opened his mouth, then shut it again, mutely watching Michael's approach. He didn't flinch when Michael cupped his shoulders and pulled him in close. "I want to kiss you. May I?"

Finn nodded and closed his eyes as Michael lowered his head and pressed their mouths together. He'd intended to keep it soft and light. Obviously, Finn had other ideas. Still in a passive role, Finn melted against Michael and parted his lips, inviting without demanding. Michael didn't need to be asked twice. He slid one hand up to cradle the back of Finn's head and pulled him in even closer. Deepening the kiss, he thrust his tongue inside Finn's mouth and swept every corner and surface he could find.

Finn moaned and fisted the back of Michael's shirt. Their pelvises touched, twin hard-ons rubbed through the fabric of their jeans. Michael ground against Finn and moaned at the pleasure shocking his dick. Breaking the kiss, he nipped his way down Finn's throat and growled into the crook of his neck. He wanted to taste his nipples, but the damn muscle shirt was in the way. He released his grip on Finn long enough to yank the thing off. Then he took a moment to stand and admire.

Smooth pecs with rosy taut nipples beckoned his fingers. With a light touch, he stroked and petted the soft skin, stopping to pinch and tweak the buds. Finn's eyes closed, and he made a little sound, half whimper, half groan. Michael pushed him over into full on groaning when his mouth replaced his fingers on one nipple. He laved and sucked, and when that wasn't near enough, he nibbled and scraped.

Finn shuddered. "Shit!"

Michael stilled. "Too much?"

"Not enough," Finn replied in a strangled voice. "More. Please?"

"I need you naked."

Michael didn't wait for his words to sink in or for Finn to comply. Instead, he swiped his palms down Finn's ripped abs and yanked open the snap of the enticing skinny jeans. Pulling them down was a chore. They were painted on, so he dropped to his knees, taking a moment to lick across the ridges of those abs. He was rewarded when Finn's stomach rippled in response, and his breath came out in stutter.

His next reward made his breathing hitch. Beneath the jeans, holding Finn's engorged cock tight to his body was a deep blue swath of silky cloth that, on closer inspection, was a thong.

"Oh," was all he could say as he pealed the pants down firm, almost hairless thighs.

He stopped at Finn's knees and palmed the high and taut globes of Finn's ass. He coaxed him closer so he could put his mouth right on top of the pulsing bulge that seemed to wiggle to break free. He lipped and sucked through the fabric, pulling moans from Finn. When he pressed in closer and trapped Finn's hardness between his teeth, Finn fisted his hair and urged him in farther. Michael obliged, scraping his way up to the top of the thong, then pulling it down with his teeth to free the tip of Finn's cock.

Michael opened his eyes for a second, just for the pleasure of seeing an aroused Finn. The head of Finn's dick didn't disappoint. It glistened with pre-cum and begged to be licked. Running his tongue up past the glans, he delved into the slit and Frenched it until Finn started to buck his hips against Michael's face. An explosion of breath skimmed the top of his head.

He ran his fingers up the cleft of Finn's ass, and hooking them around the tiny string that circled Finn's hips, he pulled the thong down. Now, the cock was fully free, and Michael wasted no time covering it with his mouth. He took it down to the back of his throat, feasting on it until the need for air forced him to pull up. Finn's fingers dug into his scalp, and that small bite of pain drove his arousal to greater heights. Inside his pants, his dick whined like the dog it was to be let out to play.

As delicious an appetizer as Finn's cock was, it was time to move onto the main course. Michael released the hard rod with an audible plop and quickly stripped Finn of his clothing entirely. The guy was passive throughout except for the movement of his fingers, flexing and scratching at Michael's head. Still kneeling, Michael looked up and gasped. His stomach clenched, as if he'd been kicked in the gut, when he saw the expression on Finn's face. Eyes closed and head thrown back, he was a study in ecstasy.

Michael shot to his feet to claim Finn's mouth once more. With one hand, he captured the back of Finn's head to pull him into the kiss. With the other, he squeezed Finn's tight balls and stroked his cock. He smiled against Finn's lips when he dragged a long moan from him.

Breaking the kiss, he whispered, "I need to be inside you. Get on the bed."

Finn's eyes popped open, glassy and unfocused.

"Yes, Daddy."

Michael winced at the reminder that they weren't just two men finally acting on their high octane attraction to each other. They were working, and someone was watching and listening or soon would be.

"Michael. Call me Michael," he commanded in a voice thick with his arousal. What harm could it do? There were thousands of Michaels in Boston. He wanted the illusion of it being just them. Needed it.

Finn surprised him by taking Michael's lower lip between his teeth and nipping him before answering. "Michael. How do you want me, on my hands and knees?"

Michael shook his head as he reluctantly let Finn go and propelled him toward the bed. "No, on your back. I want to see your face."

He grappled with his own clothes as they were suddenly too confining and would only separate him from the feel of Finn's completely naked body. He watched Finn intently as he lay down on the bed just as Michael had ordered. Every inch of the lean, toned body was worth his attention. Finn moved with the grace of a dancer and when he reclined, his movements clearly said "come and fuck me."

With a toss of his clothing and shoes in all different directions, Michael freed himself. His liberated cock led the way to the bed, pulsing with excitement and aching with need. He knelt down on the side with one knee and brought his hands to rest on either side of Finn's head.

Their gazes locked for long seconds until Finn broke the silence. "Don't make me wait."

Michael's pupils dilated wide enough to almost

obscure his irises as he stared down at Finn. Although his experience with other men was limited, Finn knew when another man wanted him. This wasn't just for show. The operation be damned, Michael wanted this to happen as much as Finn did. He ruthlessly shoved aside any concerns about the surveillance and who might eventually see what should have been the most private moment, something to savor for the rest of their lives. Except now, he was getting maudlin about it. This was just fucking even if it was with someone he liked. They had no future together, after all.

Michael pushed off the bed. "Do you have supplies?" There was an almost wild look to him.

Finn nodded. "Condom and lube in my backpack."

Michael hurried to grab the bag and pull out what they needed. Taking a deep breath and letting it out slowly, Finn willed his muscles to relax. Michael was in control, knew what he wanted, what they both wanted. All Finn had to do was loosen up enough to take the other man inside his body. His cock throbbed, demanding to be touched, but he refused to listen. When he came, he wanted Michael's hand on his flesh.

Michael returned to the bed with a condom already covering his impressive dick. Just as his subconscious has imagined, it was both long and thick, and Finn knew it would be hard to take. His hole quivered at the thought. He spread his legs and raised his knees as Michael slid in between them. The lube was clutched tight in one hand, but before he did anything more, Michael leaned down and kissed Finn with bruising force.

"It's just us," he whispered.

Then he sat up and rested on his heels as he

squirted a dollop of lube on a couple of fingers. He kept his gaze on Finn while he teased the outside of Finn's hole. The sensation caused Finn to squirm until Michael wrapped his free hand around one of Finn's thighs and held him still. The finger slipped inside, barely noticeable given how turned on Finn was. As Michael fucked him with it using slow strokes, Finn grunted in frustration and bucked his hips in a silent plea to move things along.

Michael shook his head slowly and kept up the steady pace. Just as Finn thought he'd go truly mad, a second finger joined the first and Finn got his first real taste of the exquisite burn of having his hole stretched. He arched his back and cried out when those fingers curled to stroke his prostate. God, it was too much and not enough. As if understanding the sweet torture he performed, Michael at least sped up the thrusting, rubbing the sensitive bundle of nerves with each passing.

Finn whimpered and moaned and writhed shamelessly until all he could do was chant, "Fuck me, fuck me. Fuck. Me!"

Suddenly the fingers were gone, and in their place was the broad head of Michael's cock. "Look at me, Finn."

Finn forced his head to still and his eyes to stay open. He kept his gaze locked on Michael's eyes. As Michael pushed his cock slowly into Finn's body, he also pushed Finn's legs forward so his knees almost touched his chest. The burning fullness of Michael's hard length sliding into his body robbed him of his breath and any thoughts other than "more."

When he was seated to the hilt, Michael let go of

Finn's thighs and dropped down so his forearms bracketed Finn's head. He kissed him long and slow while he kept his body otherwise still. He was being kind, giving Finn a chance to adjust to the invasion. Sweet, but not what Finn wanted. He wanted, no needed, hard and fast. Bucking his hips up to take the cock in deeper, he moaned as wantonly as he could into Michael's mouth.

The man chuckled and pulled back. "Message received, sweetheart."

Michael thrust, a shallow effort that seated him more firmly. Then he thrust again, this time with more momentum and force. Seconds later, he was pounding into Finn fast enough and hard enough to make the bed squeak and shimmy. Sweat formed along his brow, and everywhere their bodies touched, they were both slick.

Finn grabbed the back of his thighs to keep his legs up high and steady, giving Michael as much access to his body as possible at that angle. His cock wept between them, begging to be touched. The near constant stroking of his prostate wasn't enough, but he was too intent on having as much of Michael's dick up his ass as he could get to let go of his hold and take care of himself.

Michael knew, though. He understood Finn's need without being told. He lifted up enough to slide a hand between them and clasp Finn's cock in a firm grip. As he fucked, he stroked, bringing Finn up to the edge at the same time as he took himself. Then they were tumbling over, each of them crying out their release. Finn slammed his eyes shut and tossed his head as the orgasm rocketed through his body, flying out of his head, his fingers, his toes, and his cock. He clamped down like a vice on Michael's pulsing cock and slammed his ass against Michael's hips.

Wet warmth splashed across his stomach as Michael milked him dry. Their harsh breaths mingled in the space above Finn's face. Michael's lips fumbled around Finn's until their mouths fused and they kissed, letting their tongues work out the last of the aftershocks of their passion. Finally, too soon, Michael broke the contact and eased out of Finn. The bed creaked and bounced as Michael got up, then a few seconds later, the toilet flushed.

Finn kept his eyes shut for a couple of minutes, unable to let the fantasy of being with Michael go and face the reality of where they were and why. Easing his legs down, he stretched and catalogued his aches. Under different circumstances, he would try to coax his lover into coming back to bed and waiting for another round. This wasn't college, though, or any other kind of normal pick-up. He was on the job. So he forced his eyelids to come up and saw Michael dressed and holding a wash cloth beside the bed. Wordlessly Michael passed the cloth to Finn, who took it and wiped semen off his stomach and chest.

He got dressed in a hurry and made sure the lube was back in his pack before he dared to look Michael in the eye. The guy wore a bittersweet expression as he stared back. Then he pulled out his wallet and handed Finn a wad of cash that was easily twice what Elvis had quoted him. When Finn gave him a quizzical look back, Michael shrugged.

"Take it. You deserve it. I, uh, appreciate how you made this a really nice fantasy. I don't, you know, do this sort of thing very often, and well, it felt like you really were into me and that matters."

Taking the money and stuffing it into his backpack, Finn felt himself blush. Why did it seem as if Michael's words were more than just for the surveillance? As he peered into the man's eyes, Finn was sure there was a message for him and him alone. Of course, by his own admission, Michael was almost celibate. Maybe this encounter really did mean something special to him. He needed to know it was the same for Finn.

Closing the gap between them, Finn reached up and gave Michael a quick kiss. "Thank you, Michael. This was good for me, too. Seriously, you're a nice guy."

With nothing more to say, Finn turned and left the room with Michael in his wake. He dropped the key off with the clerk who looked up from his reading material long enough to smirk and waggle his tongue at Finn. Hiding his disgust, Finn walked outside and found Elvis waiting for him. The boy's eyebrows winged up, but Finn ignored him for a second to say good-bye to Michael. All he saw was the man's retreating back. The dismissal stung for about two seconds before he slapped himself mentally. All this billing and cooing would get Elvis suspicious.

"So, my man, how did it go?"

Finn switched his attention back to Elvis and discreetly pulled out the money Michael had given him. "He gave me extra."

Elvis's eyes popped as he grabbed the bills and shoved them into his pocket. "Wow, that's awesome. Way to go, Finn." He patted him on the back. "Hey, are you okay?"

Not really. I just got fucked by a guy I really like

and it's forever tainted by your asshole Boss and his shitty prostitution ring. "I'm fine, why?"

Elvis winced. "'Cause you're kind of crying."

Finn swiped at his face with one hand and realized the boy was right. He hadn't noticed tears sliding down his cheeks. Fuck! "It's nothing. I guess I'm just wigged out or something. He didn't hurt me or anything."

As embarrassed as he was by being so emotional, he decided to see if it could work to his advantage. "Um, do you think that's enough for Rizzo tonight? I'm kind of sore and tired. Can't I go back to the house? I promise I'll do more tomorrow." He put a note of pleading in his voice and gave Elvis the most vulnerable look he could manage.

The boy huffed and sighed. "Yeah, okay. You did good, man. I'll make it square with Rizzo. You just be sure to work that pretty ass of yours twice as hard tomorrow. Deal?"

Finn gave him a watery smile that was only half faked. "Deal."

He'd bought himself some time while still proving himself to the ring. That goodwill would only last so long, however. God only knew what would happen the next night. His cock pulsed once as a vision of Michael taking him again popped up. But, no, no way. They couldn't risk the same guy seeking him out night after night. It wouldn't be enough anyway. Sooner or later, he was going to have to service strange men. If he didn't, they'd never let him near the head of this loathsome snake. He could do it. He could do anything it took to save those boys he was going back to face.

Chapter Seven

Michael looked down at the caller I.D. with an annoyance that didn't abate when he saw who was on the line. "Hey, LT, what's up?" He tried to make his tone sound like he was interested in the answer and paying attention to it, neither of which was true. His focus, as always in the last few days, was on Finn and on what little they could glean from their surveillance of the house he was being kept in.

"Two things, Caruso." There was enough edge to the lieutenant's voice to make Michael take notice. "One is the commissioner just left my office asking for an update on your op and in particular the state of Finn Callaghan's health."

Michael frowned. "Wait, what, sir? How does the commissioner know about all this?"

A harsh breath blew through the phone. "Because he's the fucking police commissioner, Caruso. He knows everything even when no one intends for him to. Plus, he's an old friend of Callaghan's father. The kind that used to hold little Finn on his lap and read him bedtime stories. In fact, he referred to Callaghan as his Godson and given that the commissioner's name is Finnegan, I'm thinking Finn's his namesake. So I would imagine he keeps tabs on all of the Callaghans as a matter of course and Finn in particular. He was not happy to be out of the loop and emphasized in a subtle yet clear way that my personal ass is on the line if this op goes sideways and anything happens to precious Finn Callaghan. And needless to say, if my ass is in trouble, so is yours."

What a douche! Not the lieutenant who was a good cop and leader who stood behind his people. It was the commissioner that he had a problem with, making a good man sweat, as if he were the only one worried about Finn's safety. There was little else on Michael's mind twenty-four seven. Michael was pretty sure no one on the whole planet was more worried about Finn than Michael was.

Huh. He chewed on that thought for a few seconds as the lieutenant continued his understandable rant. Sometime, undoubtedly the moment his cock had slid into Finn's warm and willing body, Michael's perception of the other man had changed. The desire for Finn had been there from the first second he'd set eyes on him. There was just more to it since that night. He'd walked away from Finn outside the seedy hotel, fighting the urge to turn and look again and again. He didn't merely care about Finn as an undercover rookie he was responsible for. He cared about him, period.

"The other reason I called is more pertinent to your op."

Michael forced his head back in the game. "What's that, sir?"

"A Ms. Brown called and left a message. One of the boys you rescued wants to speak with you."

"Craig?"

"Anderson, right. She left her number. I'll text it to you."

"Thanks, LT."

"Things are going well, aren't they?"

"Yes, sir. We're getting close."

"Good."

Michael hung up and waited for the text to come through. He turned his attention back to the voices coming through the audio transmitter. It was just a few boys goofing around before the night came and they were sent out to peddle their asses. Their handler, Rizzo, was up in his room with one boy doing God knew what, and none of them had the stomach to try and listen. There would be plenty of evidence to convict the fucker once Finn led them to the head man. In the meantime, they all had to grit their teeth and swallow their bile.

His phone pinged with the number, and he dialed it. The idea that Craig had more information for him was encouraging, but he hated to leave given the lateness of the day. Finn would be leaving with the others. He never went to the same location twice, and so far always with Elvis leading the way. They didn't trust Finn not to run yet. Because Michael didn't dare rouse suspicion by dogging their heels, others had had to take his place, although fortunately Finn hadn't been made to go to the room under surveillance again. Apparently what the ring had seen from his and Finn's performance had convinced them he was playing ball well enough.

It also meant Finn was supposed to bring in a lot more money by servicing more guys. Not unexpected, and Michael had already lined his two tech guys to go in. Nerdy as they were, they'd bumbled through the transaction very convincingly, too shy and embarrassed to be made as cops. Then Ronan had stepped up to the plate, a disturbing scenario on so many levels. Michael had worried as well that Ronan looked so much like his brother he wouldn't be taken as a stranger. Of course, the guy was the man of a thousand faces, so that proved to be unfounded. Without anyone watching, it also allowed Ronan the opportunity to debrief Finn while they were supposed to be fucking.

After that, Finn had a healthy line of clients, just enough to keep Rizzo happy but not enough to be suspicious. All of those men were friends of Ronan or acquaintances of the man. Not cops he'd said, just guys that owed him a favor or two. He swore they knew nothing about the operation. They simply accepted Ronan's request to hire a boy whore and only pretend he'd serviced them. Those were some tight friends to have, or Ronan held something over them to make them compliant. Either way, the whole idea had made Michael uncomfortable, yet it'd worked, at least so far. This couldn't go on much longer, though.

"Ellie Brown."

"Michael Caruso, Ms. Brown. I got word Craig wants to talk to me again?"

"Yes, he was very agitated when he contacted me. He's anxious to see you as soon as possible."

Michael took a moment to weigh the importance of meeting the boy and leaving Finn for a few hours. Of course, Finn was in good hands, and Craig might have critical information. There really was no choice, except. "Will he talk to me over the phone?"

"Sorry, no. He insists on telling you in person. You have to understand he's traumatized and sees danger in everything and everyone. It's amazing to me how well he responds to you, given you're a man in particular."

"I understand and appreciate his confidence in me. When and where?"

He agreed to meet in an hour at the place Craig was being housed and had Ronan pick him up in the old beater. Ronan dropped him off at his car parked blocks away and he arrived at the facility just as Brown was entering the building. She shot him a tired smile.

"I need to be here when you question him even if he did initiate it."

"I understand." He held the door open for her. "How's he doing?"

"As well as can be expected. I wish they could find a home for him. It would help I think if he were somewhere more normal. Not that he isn't being well cared for. It's just…" Her voice trailed off.

"I get it. And an abused gay teenager is not at the top of anybody's list of what they're looking for in a kid."

"Unfortunately."

They waited in the same room as before. Craig came in with a little more confidence than the last time. He wore a short-sleeved T-shirt, and Michael was happy to see the bruises had faded.

He shot the boy a smile. "Hi, Craig. How're you doing?"

Craig shrugged his shoulders as he sat down. "Okay, I guess."

"Good. I guess," Michael said in deliberate imitation of the boy's tone, and it elicited a small smile as he'd intended. "You wanted to tell me something?"

The boy's gaze lifted to Michael, and there was still a lot of fear and hurt in them. "Yeah, I remembered something more, and I know it's important to tell you everything."

"It is, absolutely. What is it?"

Craig wore at a scar on the table with his finger for a few seconds. "The guy who was bagged and sent off to be fucked by that Boss dude?"

Brown winced at the description, but she didn't say anything. Michael gave her a sympathetic look before answering Craig. "What about him?"

"I remember he said the dude's house was kind of skinny."

"Skinny?"

"Yeah, it went up a lot of floors, but there wasn't much to them, a couple of rooms, is all, maybe. He said it was weird 'cause rich means having a big house."

Townhouse. Back Bay, perhaps. "Okay, that's really helpful. Anything else?"

"Maybe. He said after the guy fucked him, he stood at his window with binoculars. And this kid said he laughed 'cause he was high on weed and booze he said Boss gave him. Anyway, he asked Boss what kind of birds he saw at night, and the dude said he was looking at the college boys who were too stupid to close their blinds." Craig shrugged again. "I guess it was across from a college or something."

"Student housing," Michael said under his breath. There were a lot of colleges in Boston, and many of them owned older houses they had converted into dorms.

He gave Craig a big smile. "That's good. Really helpful. Anything else?"

Craig shook his head. "Naw, that's it. I just. I'd really like to get out of here. I know I need a place to go and I don't have one, so…"

Brown patted him once on the hand, pulling back immediately when Craig flinched and snatched his hand away. "We're working on it, Craig. I promise we are."

"Forget it. It's fine," the boy murmured when everyone in the room knew it wasn't fine at all.

Fucking A, Michael wished there was something he could do. As there wasn't, he needed to concentrate on what he could do. Standing up, he stuck his hand out as he had before with Craig to show him thanks and respect and to make sure he knew that, despite everything that had been done to him, he was not tainted.

Craig clasped his hand briefly. "No, problem, man." As he shuffled over to the door, shoulders hunched as if weighed down by their talk and not buoyed by it, he stopped and looked over at Michael. "You're gonna get these assholes, right?"

"You can count on it. I promise."

Although the boy's smile didn't quite meet his eyes, it was a start.

****

Finn pretended he didn't understand what Rizzo was saying. "I'm going to some guy's house tonight instead of working the street?"

"Not just a house, the house," Elvis said before Rizzo could respond.

"Did I say I needed your help?" Rizzo barked out.

Elvis hung his head. "No, sir. Sorry."

Rizzo gave Finn a toothy grin. At this point, Finn knew how false that cheer was. "This is a special man, someone we all owe a thanks to. He likes pretty boys, boys who know how to make a man happy. You're all that and a bag of chips."

Seriously? Who said that anymore? He mentally slapped himself. As if Rizzo's goofy speech was as important as the prospect of meeting Boss. And it had to be that man. Who else could Rizzo mean?

He licked his lips. "Um, okay, sure. I mean one guy doing me for the night? That sounds cool. What, um, what does he want?"

"He'll let you know, don't worry. Elvis and I will be driving you there in a few hours, once it's nice and dark. Until then, you can hang out, save up your energy."

"Hey, Rizzo, is it okay if Finn and I make a run to the packy and maybe get a snack or something?" Elvis asked.

Rizzo squinted at Elvis, as if gauging the risk of the request before nodding. "Sure. Just be back in time. We don't keep this man waiting, ever."

"No problem, man. Come on," he said, shoving Finn from the room.

"What's going on?" Finn asked once they were out of the house.

"I need a drink, is what's going on," Elvis replied with a huff. "This man you're going to party with tonight is a big fucking deal around here. He makes Rizzo sweat, you hear me?" He glanced at Finn, who nodded. "Makes me sweat, too, except I can't touch Rizzo's beer unless I suck him off, and I don't feel like sucking him off today, so we go to the packy and get a nip or two. They don't cost much. I can cover it with what little Rizzo pays me."

As they hustled down the street, Finn kept his eyes out for anyone familiar. He knew Michael and his team were in a house behind Rizzo's. Ronan had told him as much as they'd sat in a hotel room pretending to fuck. And thinking about his brother as his john, even a pretend one, was going to drive him into therapy if he dwelled on it any more. A familiar figure rounded the corner and shuffled in their direction. Wash.

"You can't have any," Elvis broke into Finn's concentration. "If the man smells any alcohol on your breath, they'll find my body floating in the Charles. I hear he gives boys booze and weed, though, so you got that to look forward to."

As they and Wash reached each other, the older man stepped into their path, forcing them to stop.

"Get out of our face, man. We're Rizzo's boys, you hear me?"

"Rizzo don't mean shit to me, boy," Wash sneered.

"You must be new to this neighborhood, so I'll cut you some slack and not say anything." When Elvis tried to keep going, Wash blocked his way. Elvis glared up at him, but given Wash's size, the smaller man didn't try to shove past.

"This pretty white ass for rent or what?" Wash asked, his eyes raking Finn.

Elvis snorted. "Not for your drugged up dick."

Reaching into the pocket of his greasy pants, Wash discretely flashed a wad of bills. "I got bank. Just want a half hour at my place."

Wash grinned to show teeth that looked like they hadn't been brushed in a few weeks. In fact, the cop smelled like he'd been living in his clothes for even longer. Which was the whole point, of course. It was easy for Finn to show his disgust at the idea.

"Come on, Elvis. Let's go," he urged.

"Hold on," Elvis hissed back. "Two hundred up

front for thirty minutes, and you better double bag that tool of yours.”

Wash nodded and handed the money over to Elvis. “No, problem.” He reached for Finn’s arm.

Finn yanked it away from him. “Don’t touch me!”

Wash laughed. “Oh, pretty little white boy, I’m going to touch you a whole lot more when I get you home.”

Finn turned pleading eyes on Elvis. “You can’t be serious.”

“Hey, man, don’t be like that about a client.” Leaning closer, he murmured, “You think every john’s going to be like that hot guy you got the other night? Now be cool, and I’ll share the money with you. Rizzo don’t have to know about it. Hiding money away means you have a better chance of going off on your own one day.” His eyes got narrow and hard. “You don’t say nothing to Rizzo, you understand?”

Finn choked back a whimper. “Okay, I get it. I’ll do it. I get half, though, right?”

Elvis gave him a broad grin. “Absolutely.”

Glaring up at Wash, Finn said, “No touching me until we get to your place and then only as much as is necessary to get your dick into my ass.”

Wash made a kissing sound. “Sure thing, sweetheart.”

With a last glance at Elvis, Finn followed Wash back down the street.

****

“What the fuck!” Michael stopped dumfounded inside the doorway. Finn stood with his shirt pulled up and his pants pulled down. One of the tech guys kneeled in front of him, his head bent close to Finn’s crotch.

"He's not giving him a blowjob," Wash remarked from over to one side.

"Good. I'd have to crack some skulls if that were the case," Ronan said from over Michael's shoulder. With a not so gentle shove, he moved Michael farther into the room so he could enter.

Ever since the night Finn had been turned out by being fucked by Michael, Ronan had had an extra hint of mean in his look and tone. Of course, everyone knew what had gone down. In an operation like this, it wasn't possible or safe to hide things from team members. He'd told Ronan himself because, he believed he owed the guy that much and had fully expected a crack to his jaw. Ronan had surprised him by merely grunting and walking away.

"You're wiring him?" Michael asked, moving to a position that allowed him so see better what the techie was doing.

"Yup, tracking chip, actually," the guy confirmed. "Given what he's expected to wear, there's only his groin to place it in so it can't been seen."

Michael grimaced when he realized the guy was taping the small chip to a place that had closely cropped pubic hair. That was going to hurt when it came off. Finn looked up at him from under his lashes. It was the first time they'd seen each other since the night in the hotel. There was a buzz and a crackle in the air, as if lightning was about to strike, although no one seemed to notice except him. And maybe Finn, who quickly looked away again.

"How'd you manage to get away for this?" Although he'd directed the question to Finn, Wash answered.

"We heard Rizzo give him marching orders for tonight. He's going to meet Boss."

"Thank fuck." Michael shut his eyes a moment in a kind of relief. "So again, how'd he end up here?"

"Elvis convinced Rizzo to let us get out of the house for a while. Wash met us on the street." Finn gave the answer just as the tech guy finished up. Finn pulled up his pants and let his shirt down again.

"I figured our only chance to wire Finn was now. I bought a half hour of his time."

"Apparently Elvis, and the other boys probably, do some business on the side to earn money that Rizzo doesn't know about."

"I figured that was the case as it frequently is with prostitutes," Wash said. "Gives them running money if they get the chance."

Looking at his watch, Finn said, "My times up. I better get going."

"That Elvis character is hanging around the front stoop," Ronan said as he stared at one of the monitors.

"That's my cue." Finn stood with his arms stretched out. "Can anyone see the chip?"

Every guy in the room stared hard at Finn's crotch, which was both necessary and irritating as Michael wanted to be the only one doing that. A stupid thought and one only worthy of the teenage mind with his first crush. It was there nevertheless, goading him into a snarl. Instead, he walked over to Finn and took him by the arm.

"It's fine. Come on, before Elvis becomes suspicious."

If anyone, Finn included, thought he was acting

high-handed, they didn't say anything as he pulled Finn out of the room and down the stairs. He was not so stupid as to walk Finn out the door. Stopping well away from any spot Elvis might see from outside, Michael pulled Finn up against his body and kissed him—hard and fast.

"Be careful."

Finn gave him a lazy smile. "Always. What was the kiss for, luck?"

"No, that was me telling you what happened the other night in that hotel was not just part of the op, not an act to convince the ring you are under their control. That was you and me, finishing what we started days ago in my car."

Reaching up, Finn delivered an equally hard and fast kiss. "Okay, then. I'll see you when this is all over."

Michael headed back up the stairs so Finn could open the front door without concern. But he stopped just past the landing for the second floor and peered around the corner. He caught a glimpse of Finn's back and felt a sudden and almost overwhelming desire to race down and snatch him back inside.

Instead, he did his job and returned to the command center. Everyone else's attention was glued to a monitor, watching Finn return to Rizzo's house. Everything appeared to be fine. Elvis had his arm around Finn's shoulder as he frequently did, and there was no hint of tension in Finn's body that they could see. The two boys walked into the house, then Michael and the others were back to listening in on the various conversations that could be picked up.

For the next couple of hours, as the sun set,

everything was situation normal. Michael still paced around the room like the proverbial cat on a hot tin roof. His worries about Finn were endless. What if the ring discovered the tracking chip, what if Boss tried to rape Finn before they could bust things up. What if Boss actually raped Finn before Michael could get to him. The "what ifs" were endless, and each one gave Michael a queasy stomach. He told himself they had all the bases covered and Finn was a trained police officer even though he was a rookie. He wasn't like Craig and the other boys, alone and defenseless.

It would be okay. Tonight it would end, and he and Finn would have time to explore what was growing between them. It was past time for Michael to be out completely and stop hiding behind a sadly dead girlfriend. There was nothing wrong with being gay, he knew that. For him to believe otherwise, he'd have to also believe there was something wrong with Finn. And there wasn't. The man was perfect in every way. Perfect for Michael certainly, and he'd make sure to let Finn know it as soon as he could.

"This is it," one of the tech guys said.

Michael's heart lurched in his chest as his attention snapped back to the here and now. Finn, along with Elvis and Rizzo, came out of the house and got into a black Escalade with tinted windows. No big surprise in Rizzo's choice of ride. Elvis got behind the wheel as Rizzo ushered Finn into the back seat. That struck Michael as odd. Elvis didn't look like the chauffer type and the Escalade was a big and expensive vehicle. If it had been Michael's, he wouldn't let anyone else drive it, not even Finn. Well, not at first anyway.

He was being paranoid. It meant nothing.

As the three men pulled away, Michael said, "Let's go."

He, Ronan, and the tech guys headed down to the back of their house where the surveillance van was parked. With Finn bugged, they could trail at a discreet distance. Wash stayed behind just in case something developed at the home front they'd need to know about. With Ronan driving, Michael riding shotgun, and the tech guys in back, they took off into the night.

This would all be over soon. Thank fuck.

****

Finn tried not to fidget or look like he was paying too much attention to where they were going. Weird that he wasn't blindfolded or anything. Michael had said the boys delivered to Boss had been, or at least a boy he'd interviewed thought that was the case. Rizzo sat next to him and the guy's presence unnerved him. It shouldn't have been a surprise that this delivery wasn't being left in Elvis' hands. Still, Rizzo was sharper than Elvis and he had his eyes on Finn, not on the kind of shaky way Elvis drove the big SUV.

They were getting onto the Mass Pike, and that told Finn Boss was in the burbs. Again, not such a surprise given how much money the ring must bring in. It made him even madder than he had been. Rich guy hiding out in the comfort of the upper middle class while boys were forced to sleep on cots and take a beating when they didn't sell their body enough in one night.

Rizzo startled him by switching on the interior light. "You know, Irish, you look older this close."

The hairs on the back of Finn's neck stood up. With forced calm, he turned to the other man. "Yeah? Good. I hate looking like a kid." He turned his gaze back to his side window.

The seat rippled as Rizzo slid a little closer to him. A hand descended on Finn's thigh, and Finn started with surprise.

"What are you doing?" he asked as he tried to move away. There was nowhere to go, of course, and unlike Rizzo, Finn had his seat belt on. It held him in place.

Rizzo's face broke into a nasty smile, and he squeezed his fingers. "You belong to me, Irish. I can do what I like, although you're really too old for my tastes." He slid his hand up closer to Finn's crotch.

"But, I thought I was going to service Boss." Finn didn't try to hide his mounting fear. It worked well enough for his cover, and it was damn hard to keep it under wraps.

"Oh, you are. You most definitely are," Rizzo said, getting close enough that Finn could smell the beer on his breath. "I'm just going to check you out first."

Finn couldn't stand looking into those cruel eyes. Rizzo got off on making him sweat. Finn caught Elvis' eye in the rearview mirror. He saw fear there, and something else. Regret maybe. Then his breath caught in his throat when the muzzle of a gun pressed against his cheek.

"What?" was all he managed to get out before Rizzo ran his free hand down Finn's torso, pressing into his armpits and feeling around his back. They were practically hugging, the way Rizzo pressed his body against Finn's. Finally, Rizzo snapped open Finn's jeans, shoved his fingers down into the tight space between the pants and Finn's skin.

Sharp pain stung his leg when Rizzo ripped the

chip off and pulled it out. He moved away from Finn then, although the gun stayed where it was.

Rizzo tsked. "It's a shame, Irish. I liked you. You would have made me a nice tidy sum if you'd really been a fifteen year old runaway." He lowered his window and tossed the chip out. "You know where to go, Elvis."

"Yes, sir." There was a waver to the boy's voice, but Finn didn't have time to worry about him.

He kept his gaze fixed on Elvis's headrest. With the gun at his head, there was no way for him to turn and look Rizzo in the eye. There was no reason to try to deny the truth, either.

"How did you find out?"

Rizzo chuckled. "You know, I don't even know. Boss found out and told me this morning. He wants to meet you in the worst kind of way."

"I'm surprised he has the guts to get his hands dirty," Finn said with as much contempt as he could muster. Sweat trickled down his back. He was in trouble, but even without the chip, Michael and the others had to be close. They knew the vehicle he'd been taken in. There was a chance they would find him.

"Depends on your definition of getting dirty. He wants a chance at that pretty ass of yours, for sure. Boss doesn't do consensual real well. The more the boy hates it, the better he likes it. That's been my observation anyway."

"It's not too late for you to stop this, Rizzo. We know who you are. You can't stay in Boston once you're involved in killing a cop. Boss will probably kill you. If you turn yourself in now, help us get Boss, I can help broker a deal to give you a reduced sentence."

Rizzo chuckled again, although he didn't sound particularly happy. "Yeah, I know my house is fucked, thanks to you. I ain't going back. Your cop friends are welcome to go in and take the boys, rehabilitate them or whatever the fuck you do. Boss has connections out of town, and I'm still useful to him. There are always more boys. Every fucking city in the country has them. You don't have my real identity, and I'm not in anyone's system. I've been careful. Which is more than I can say for you, Irish. So, thanks but no thanks."

There was a flash of movement before pain exploded in Finn's head. The last thing he saw were Elvis' eyes in the rearview mirror.

Chapter Eight

"Something's wrong."

Michael swiveled in his seat to stare in the back of the van. "What do you mean?"

The tech guy shook his head. "The signal is stationary after going wildly off to the side of where it was."

"And?" Michael's tone was sharp because his heart was climbing up his throat.

"And they're supposed to be just ahead of us. There's no exit on the Pike where the signal is coming from." The guy looked at Michael with big, alarmed eyes. "I think it's on the side of the road or something."

Michael didn't bother swearing. Ronan was doing that well enough for both of them.

"Are you saying they made him?" Michael's voice was close to being at roar level. He didn't care and ignored the way the other guy winced.

"I'm saying if the chip is still on Officer Callaghan, then he's not moving anymore."

Oh, fuck! Fuck! Fuck! Fuck! Not moving could mean Finn was on the side of the road, too. Not just the chip.

"Hit the siren," he ordered Ronan. The op was busted. No need for stealth.

Ronan did as commanded and hit the accelerator as well. He weaved around the relatively light traffic given the hour of the day and kept up his speed until the tech guy told him to slow down. As soon as Ronan was told to pull over, Michael jumped out of the van, a flashlight in his hand. With his heart racing fast enough to burst, he scanned the breakdown lane, then beyond it into the scrub on the side of the highway. At each passing of the beam, he feared he'd see a body.

The tech guys joined him and did the same. Nothing, thank God, nothing. The chip was out there somewhere, almost impossible to see. It didn't matter, though. It wasn't on Finn. The question was, where had they taken him and could Michael reach him before they killed him? Ronan jogged up.

"I've called Daire, and he's getting Regan. We need more people, and we know we can trust them, at least."

Michael looked at him and nodded. "The leak."

Ronan nodded back. Despite their efforts to keep the operation quiet, the wrong person on the department must have ratted Finn out. Son of a God damn bitch. When he found out who it was… No, now wasn't the time. Finding Finn was all that mattered. He fisted his hair with one hand while dialing Wash on the other.

"Yo?"

Michael's voice caught in his throat. "They made him, Wash. They know he's a cop and ripped the tracking chip off him. We don't know where he is."

Wash swore briefly before getting with the program. "What can I do?"

"Call in SWAT and raid Rizzo's house. See if there's anything to help us find where they've taken Finn."

"On it." Wash hung up.

"Okay, let's get going." He raced back to the van.

"Where do we go?" Ronan asked as he slid in behind the wheel.

Michael took a deep breath and forced himself to calm down and think clearly. His interview with Craig played through his mind. "Back Bay."

"Seriously? We're headed west of the City."

"A ruse. Boss has a townhouse and one that is located across the street from student housing. That says Back Bay to me."

"Hmm," Ronan roared back out onto the Pike and hit the siren and the gas. "Maybe. I can't think of anywhere in Brookline or Newton or Cambridge that fits better."

"Me, neither. So we try Comm Ave, Marlboro, and Beacon. Look for the Escalade."

"You think he's going to park that thing on the street, knowing we have the plate number as well as model and make?"

"Why not if he doesn't know we know where to look?"

"Right." Ronan took out his phone and called the info into Daire so he and Regan Malloy could start the search."

"Take the next exit."

Ronan shot him a look as he pocketed his phone. "I know how to turn around, Caruso. And for the record, I know you're as scared as I am."

Michael didn't say anything to that comment. What was there to say except, please God let them get to Finn in time.

****

The pounding in Finn's head kept time to the beat

of kettledrums. Or something. As the fog of unconsciousness lifted, Finn could hear a symphony playing, which made no sense. He didn't like classical music and neither did his brothers. Something was wrong. With a start, he remembered what had happened to him and where he must be. He forced his heavy eyelids to open in order to face his predicament.

The sight that greeted him was equally incongruous. He knew Rizzo and Elvis had been taking him to Boss. But this distinguished-looking man was not what Finn had pictured when he wondered who was behind the exploitation of teenage boys. Middle-aged, with short salt and pepper hair, the tanned man lounged in a wing-backed chair, wearing a silk robe. Long and naked legs daintily crossed at the knee were on display. He had a tumbler full of amber liquid in one hand and a thin cigar in the other. He was more Mad Men than Midnight Cowboy, although he did have his own Rizzo.

The man stared intently at him, taking sips of his drink and drags off the cigar. He was such a distraction that it took a few seconds for Finn to appreciate his situation—naked and tied to a chair. It was a really nice chair, well-padded and sturdy. The whole room reeked of money, of course. The asshole had made tons of it off boys' bodies. A quick and furtive tug told him he wasn't going to be able to free himself. Shit.

As the man didn't seem to be in any hurry to start a conversation, Finn did. "I take it you're who they call Boss?" Damn, his voice was raspy. He coughed to clear it.

The man poured out a low puff of smoke. "Yes, I am." It was a cultured voice, faked perhaps, but well-suited to his lair. "Richard Boss, actually."

Really? All this time, and Boss truly was a name and not a title. Michael was going to kick himself when he found out. If he found out. And it wasn't a good sign the man was blithely giving Finn the information. If Michael and the others didn't find him, he was dead.

Boss cocked his head. "And you are Officer Finn Callaghan."

"How do know that?"

A faint smile ghosted over his lips. "I have friends everywhere. They're easy to cultivate when you know how."

"Bribes," Finn spit out.

"Hmm, and blackmail. You'd be shocked I'm sure to learn how many upstanding men like to fuck boys while their wives are off at some charity event."

"And you record it all," Finn remarked, remembering his time with Michael at the hotel. It made him sick to think this asshole had seen the footage.

As if sensing his thoughts, the man brought it up. "You had me fooled, you know. That encounter with what I assume was another cop. Very hot." He licked his lips obscenely. "Delicious."

So that's where Rizzo got the expression. It had seemed highbrow for the gutter rat. Speaking of which. Finn risked making his head ache more by looking around. Rizzo lounged against a wall, a smirk on his face. He couldn't see Elvis. Finn took a furtive deep breath to try to settle his heartbeat.

"You're right. He's a cop. There are lots of cops on this operation. They're looking for me."

"My dear boy, they won't find you. They have no idea where I am. We can comfortably spend the night getting to know each other better.”

“Fuck you,” Finn replied, happy his voice was steady.

The man’s gleaming white teeth showed with his broad smile. “My very thought. Only I’m afraid I won’t be nearly as careful with you as your lover cop was. And first, I want to impress on you just how irritated I am at your interference with my business.”

He nodded toward Rizzo, who sauntered up to Finn, cracking his knuckles like some B movie thug. With a flick of his hand, the man did something to increase the volume of the music.

“Go ahead and scream, dear boy. No one is going to hear you.”

Finn shut his mouth in a firm line, determined to not give the bastard the satisfaction of making any noise if possible. Glaring up at a grinning Rizzo, he braced himself for the first blow. It came with lightning-fast speed and snapped his head back. The explosion of pain, mingling with the throbbing already there, made him grunt despite his efforts at stoicism.

A sound like a whimper burst out, but that wasn’t him. The man shifted his gaze somewhere farther into the room. “Keep quiet or you’re next, stupid boy. You’re the one who brought the viper into our nest, don’t forget. I certainly haven’t.”

Elvis. The kid was in trouble. Finn couldn’t worry about him, though. He had enough on his own plate. He had to hold on until Michael found him. He would. Finn had to believe it. Closing his eyes, he pictured Michael as he looked when he bent down to kiss Finn the last time. Imagined the feel of Michael’s lips on his own. He kept that vision and that sensation in his mind as the next blow landed.

And for the one after that. And for each one as Rizzo beat him bloody.

****

"Go around, fucker," Michael said under his breath as yet another car honked at their slow moving van.

They'd killed the siren once they'd returned to the city. They looked like any other van with tinted windows, albeit creeping along Marlboro Street. Daire and Regan paralleled them on Comm Ave. and Beacon Street, respectively. Everyone was searching for the Escalade and at Michael's orders, the tech guys had the surveillance equipment trained on the row of townhouses to their right. It was a desperate move, hoping to pick up some sound that showed them where Finn was.

"We don't have a warrant for this," one of the tech guys had said.

"Your point being?" Michael had shot back. The guy just shrugged and went about his work.

As if Michael was going to worry about the legalities of warrantless eavesdropping when Finn's life was on the line. They couldn't even be sure this was the right place to look. It made sense, but it was still little more than a crap shoot.

"I've reached the end of my street and turning to hit the other side," Daire said over Ronan's phone. He'd dialed in the other two on a conference call and had them on speaker.

"Me, too," Regan chimed in. Michael had never met the woman, but she was a cop and a Callaghan more or less, so that was good enough for him.

"Roger, that." Ronan glanced at Michael. "If they

are here, the guy could have his own parking garage. Some of these places do."

"That's why we've got ears on."

Michael spotted a couple of young guys carrying backpacks, taking a flight of stairs into a building across the street. "Slow down."

"Seriously, I'm doing like ten miles an hour already."

"Slow down!" Turning in his seat, he said to the tech guys, "Keep those ears on the buildings here. Focus on the higher floors. There's no way they'd keep Finn on a first floor."

The one with the headphones on shook his head, his face a study in concentration. Then, "Wait!"

Ronan slammed on the brakes a few feet past the point where the surveillance was trained.

Michael practically climbed over the seat. "What? What do you hear?"

The guy shook his head again, then nodded it. Pulling off the headphones, he tossed them over to Michael. With hands a little shaky, Michael slipped them on and closed his eyes to listen better. He heard a muffled sound, then another. A groan, maybe. His gut tightened as he strained to hear. Then a voice and the words made his blood freeze.

"What a sturdy boy you are. Not so pretty now." More muffled sounds. "Still good enough to fuck."

Whipping the headphones off, Michael pulled out his gun and shoved his door open in one continuous motion. He was halfway to the front stoop when Ronan caught up with him and yanked him to a halt by grabbing his arm. Michael tried to pull away. Ronan held fast.

"What the fuck are you doing?" Michael hissed. "Finn's up there."

"I get that!" Ronan bit out in an equally low voice. "Daire and Regan are on their way, and I've called in for more back-up and EMTs. We won't help Finn if we get killed. Here, put this on so no one shoots you."

Every fiber of Michael's being told him to race in. But Ronan was right. Grabbing the windbreaker with Boston Police written on the back, he said, "We only wait for the other two, no one else."

"Agreed."

As Ronan said it, two more cars came up fast, one was coming down the wrong way. That one was driven by a tall and lean woman with a cap of red hair. She and Daire both were pulling on their jackets as they ran to him and Ronan. Everyone put their gun at the ready as they turned to the house.

"We go in hot," Michael said. "I'm going to ring the bell. If someone answers, I'll kick the door all the way in."

"And if they don't?" Daire asked.

"We smash one of the windows."

"SWAT's on its way, and they do have a battering ram, you know," Regan pointed out.

"I don't think Finn has that kind of time."

Michael didn't wait for any reaction. Instead, he ran up the stoop and hiding his gun behind his back, he rang the bell. His nerves jangled with enough intensity he practically jumped out of his skin and his foot itched with the desire to kick the door in. A stupid idea given how sturdy it looked. He'd only bust something on himself, and that wouldn't help Finn in the least.

After another ring, he saw through the mullioned

glass panel of the door the blurry outline of a man approaching. The guy hadn't managed to open up more than an inch before Michael gave full rein to his impulses and shoved his way inside. The man, dressed in the white coat of a houseboy, went flying against the wall of the narrow hallway.

With his gun up and at the ready, Michael announced that he was the police. The stunned man leaned on a decorative table for support, his middle-aged face furrowed in confusion. Michael felt badly about roughing him up until the guy reached inside his coat for a weapon.

Before Michael could act, a body flew past him. A long leg whipped out and kicked the houseboy in the head before he could free his gun. Regan had the man on his stomach with his hands behind his back in the blink of an eye.

"Got him, go!" she hissed.

Michael's legs moved even as his brain registered the order. Ronan and Daire ran behind him as he tore up the narrow staircase to the second floor. As he rounded into the first room, a flash of someone caught his eye. He turned with gun raised and saw Elvis cringing against the wall with his hands up.

"I'm not carrying," he cried out in a voice laced with fear. "But Rizzo and Boss are. They've got Finn upstairs."

Michael's stride barely hitched as he kept turning to take the next flight.

"This one's mine," Daire said. "Face down on the ground. Arms behind your head."

Ronan was a step behind Michael as they reached the third floor. By silent agreement, Michael entered the room from the left, Ronan from the right. Two shots rang out by Michael's ear and a cry echoed in the room. Michael didn't have to look to know Rizzo, the fucker, was down and out. That left Boss, and as Elvis had said, the man was also armed. The scene he presented caused Michael's lungs to freeze.

The man who'd led him a pretty chase for more than a year stood at one end of the room, tall and elegant, his silk robe partially open to obscenely reveal his erection. Michael could have met the man anywhere and never have seen him for the monster he was. Hiding in plain sight among the rich of Boston. No wonder he had connections to protect himself enough to keep his horrible business going.

And he had Finn, naked and kneeling on the floor. His lover's beautiful face was swollen and bloody, one eye shut with an open gash on the cheek below it. Bruises already bloomed on his stomach and chest. They'd worked him over good, and Michael hoped Ronan hadn't killed Rizzo because he wanted to do it himself. But he didn't have the luxury of entertaining murderous fantasies. Boss held Finn up by one hand, clutching a hank of Finn's hair.

Worse, much worse, his gun was pressed against Finn's head.

"Well, I underestimated you," Boss drawled.

Michael gave him a feral grin. "Yes, you did, you sick fuck. "Let Officer Callaghan go."

In response to the command, the guy tightened his grip and tugged Finn's head back. Finn let out a small moan that tore at Michael's heart.

"We have something of a standoff, don't we?" asked Boss.

Michael slowly shook his head. "No, we don't. Your house is overrun by cops and more are on the way. All of your men have been neutralized one way or the other. There's nowhere for you to go, nothing for you to negotiate with."

With a yank of Finn's hair, the man said, "Nothing?"

Although it killed him, Michael repeated. "Nothing. We won't let you out of here. You kill Officer Callaghan and that just adds to your sentence."

The man shrugged. "A life sentence without parole is a life sentence without parole. What do I care how many more years they add to it? His gaze raked Michael's body. "I saw you fuck him. That wasn't some show you put on for the camera. You wanted him, not just his body, but him. You still do. You don't want me to hurt him any more than I have, do you?"

Michael didn't so much as blink at the baiting, although his gut clenched at the knowledge this piece of garbage had seen something that should have been private and beautiful between him and Finn. The fear of Finn being killed turned said guts to water, but he had to stand firm. Even if he let Boss out of the house with Finn, SWAT would take him out before he took more than a step outside. Either way, Finn was in the middle. Better, safer, for this nightmare to end in this room.

"Let go of Officer Callaghan, put the gun down slowly on the floor, and step away with your hands up."

The two men stared at each other for long seconds. It would have been a juvenile game of chicken if the stakes hadn't been so high. Finally, Boss let go of Finn, who slumped down to the floor. Then he stepped away still holding the gun. With his free hand, he reached for a tumbler on a table. He kept his gaze on Michael, his gun waist high and deadly as ever, while he downed the inch or so of liquid in the glass.

"It was a good run," Boss said with a wistful sigh, and putting the gun to his mouth, pulled the trigger.

"No!" Michael shouted as Boss's head exploded into gory pieces and his body tumbled over. "Fucking coward," he muttered as he secured his gun and raced over to Finn.

Dropping to his knees, he placed his hand gently on Finn's head. Finn shook and moaned under even that simple touch.

"Shh," Michael soothed. "It's okay, you're safe."

He twisted to see how Finn's arms were tied and swore when he saw plastic cuffs cutting into his wrists. He looked up to find Ronan, who was hovering over what he assumed was Rizzo's dead body, although his gaze was fixed on Finn.

"I need a knife or something to cut him free." When Ronan didn't respond right away, Michael barked. "Ronan, knife!"

The man jerked and raised glazed eyes to Michael. Of course the guy would be as shook up as Michael. This was his baby brother. Still, cop that he was, Ronan pulled himself together to give Michael a Swiss army knife from his pocket. The blade inside was just big enough to cut through the plastic with the right force. The effort caused Finn to groan again, and Michael thought he might cry at the notion of causing him more pain.

"It's okay, baby. I've got you," Michael crooned. "EMTs are here," he added as he became aware of the sirens and commotion outside and inside the house.

Yanking off his jacket, he placed it over Finn's lower half to give him a modicum of privacy before God and everyone came rushing in. Two seconds later, Ronan handed him his jacket to wrap around Finn's upper body. Michael cradled Finn in his arms as he did so.

With the eye that wasn't completely shut, Finn looked up at him. "Knew you'd come," he said in a hoarse voice.

The tears that had threatened earlier welled up and spilled over. "Of course, I came. I—I'm sorry, I failed you. I'm sorry you got hurt. I fucked up."

Finn managed to roll his good eye. "Don't be stupid. Not your fuck up." He coughed on the last word and winced as he did so.

"Shh, don't try to talk."

"Stop crying," Finn countered, and the irritated tone gave Michael some relief. He couldn't be too badly hurt.

"I can't seem to do that," Michael said with a watery laugh.

For a few seconds, they were in their own little world, seeing only each other. Michael tried to convey everything he felt in that short time they had. He didn't think he succeeded if only because he wasn't sure how to express his feelings even to himself. Suddenly, the room was filled with a whole lot more people, and Finn was carefully handed over to the professionals. Michael hated, absolutely hated, letting him go. But he did. It was best for Finn, and now that he had found him, there would be all the time in the world to devote to him.

****

Finn fought his way back to the surface above the

139

floaty depths of the drugs in his system. He liked the way his pain was blocked but didn't like being rendered unconscious and stupid by them. As he forced his eyelids open, he knew what he'd see. It was the same thing, same person, that he'd seen every other time he'd woken from the stupor.

Michael.

Michael had held him in his arms on the floor in the beautiful Back Bay home bought with the misery of exploited children. Michael had been there in the ambulance as the EMTs talked over his body and stuck needles into him. Michael had been there in the emergency room once the doctors finished their preliminary exam. Michael had held his hand as they wheeled him down to have a CAT scan and held it when they wheeled him back. And Michael had been sitting by his bed each and every time Finn had woken up.

Michael.

He sat with his chin cupped in one palm while his other hand clasped Finn's on the bed. His eyes were closed. Of course, he must be exhausted. They'd been in the hospital for hours, most of the night. A quick glance at the window told Finn it was still dark out, not yet morning, but it must be close to it. Finn gave himself a few minutes to lie there and drink in his fill of the man who'd saved his life and stolen his heart. Yeah, he was in love, and it wasn't just the drugs talking or the heightened emotion of nearly losing his life.

Michael Caruso had worked his way under Finn's skin. The question was, what to do about it. Michael had been clear about the limits of his sexuality. Even now, it seemed strange to him that Michael had been so open about his feelings for Finn. To touch him as much as he had in front of others meant he was willing to be openly gay. Finn had known that anyway when Michael had blurted it out to Daire so many days ago. Could he be open enough to have a relationship was the issue.

Michael's eyes fluttered open as Finn pondered his next steps. As soon as he saw Finn was awake, he straightened up and tightened his grip for a second. "Hey, how are you feeling?"

Although Finn wanted to lie and say fine, he knew that honesty was always a good starting point in a relationship, if they were going to have one. "Like shit."

Michael grimaced. "I'm not surprised." He brought their joined hands up to kiss Finn's knuckles. "I'm just glad nothing's broken or ruptured. You should be out of here later today or early tomorrow."

Finn made the same face. "I'd like to get out of here."

"Forget it," Michael advised with a shake of his head. "You have a concussion, remember? They're keeping you in for observation, and there's no arguing with that."

Finn sighed. "I suppose. Even if I wanted to get out of here, you and my brothers would only drag me back."

"And Regan, don't forget her. You should have seen the flying roundhouse kick she delivered to the armed houseboy. You don't want to cross her."

Because Michael was doing his best to lighten the mood, Flynn played along. "Yeah? You're preaching to the choir, Caruso. Regan's been beating me up since we were kids."

He ran his thumb across Michael's hand. This small touch made him ridiculously happy. "You got all of them, didn't you?"

"The kids or the pimps? Wait, stupid follow up question. We got all of them, or we're in the process of making sure we did. The tech guys are still going through computers and paper files. It may take a while to be sure we have everyone involved in the ring."

"What about Elvis?"

"He's in custody."

"I figured. It's just that he was once one of those preyed-upon boys, and he never touched me. It was all Rizzo."

"I know, and when we busted in, he surrendered and warned us the others were armed. He gets points for that."

"I want to help him if I can, testify on his behalf. I know he needs to pay for turning the corner into being a pimp. I just don't think he should be treated like Rizzo."

"Who, thanks to Ronan, is as dead as a fucking door nail."

"Good. I'm glad about Boss, too. Hey, did you know that was his actual last name?" Finn frowned. "Or did I dream that?"

Michael grimaced. "Yeah, I heard. I would never have thought he had them call him by his real name. Arrogant asshole."

"Agreed. Anyway, dead is what he deserved even if it was by his own hand. Elvis is different, though."

Michael nodded. "Okay, he's different. We'll do what we can for him."

"Thanks. What about the leak in the department?

That's how my cover got blown, wasn't it?"

A look of murderous rage crossed Michael's face for a brief second. "We can only assume so, but we don't know who it is. I doubt there's any trail for us to follow, either. God, I hope there is because I want to take whoever it is apart slowly."

Now, it was Finn who brought their hands up to kiss Michael's fingers. He ignored the twinge of pain from his split lip. "What matters is you found me."

"Yeah, thanks to Craig, a boy I rescued a few weeks back. The kid remembered things that others said about Boss to clue me into the Back Bay." He shuddered. "Fuck, it was a near thing, Finn." His voice cracked, and he looked away, wiping at his face with his other hand. "Sorry. I don't seem to be able to keep myself under control."

"Hey, it's okay." A lump formed in Finn's throat, and his one good eye filmed over with tears. "God, we're a pair, aren't we."

Michael sniffed and smiled. "We are that, definitely a pair. That is, if you're interested." He lowered his gaze.

"Interested, as in am I interested in becoming involved with you? More involved, that is."

Michael took a deep breath and looked up. "That's what I'm asking."

"I've wanted you since the moment you stepped into my house. With the op done, I'm more than ready to do something normal with you, like go on a date. And, you know, maybe fuck without anyone watching," he added with his own shyness creeping in.

"I like that plan."

"Good." Finn broke eye contact for a while as he

worked up the courage to mention the elephant in the room. "Is that going to be a problem for you? I mean, I know you've stuck to my side throughout this whole thing, and that has to be tough being so out in front of everyone. But are you okay with having an open relationship with me?"

Michael swore quietly, and for a horrible moment, Finn thought he'd killed their relationship before it had started. "Yes," Michael said firmly.

"Really?"

"Definitely. Being only half out of the closet was cowardly of me. Just like Boss blowing his brains out instead of facing his punishment." When Finn tried to interrupt, Michael said, "Let me make this confession, please." He blew out a breath. "Jesus, where to start?"

He pulled his chair in closer to the bed and clasped Finn's hand between both of his. "Back in high school, when I was still hoping I wasn't really gay, I dated this great girl. Sofia. She was a neighborhood girl, our families knew each other, and it seemed like the perfect fit. Except, of course, I didn't want her the way she deserved to be wanted. I tried, I really did. I kissed her and tried to feel her up.

"She let me, and just about every other guy in school would have been in heaven because of it." He shrugged. "For me, it was just okay. It didn't even make me hard. When I thought of touching the boy who sat next to me in history class, though, Vince? That made me hard and then some."

"A lot of guys go through a denial stage and date girls," Finn reminded him.

"I know. The thing is, Sofia and I dated for over a year, and the longer we went, the more I knew I wasn't ever going to love Sofia and appreciate her the way she deserved. I never got a chance to explain to her why I was such a lousy boyfriend. She got hit by a car while crossing the street."

"Shit."

"Yeah. Massive brain trauma. She died without every regaining consciousness. Her family was a wreck, and so was I. In my own way, I'd loved her. Anyway, it didn't seem right to come out after that. I waited and waited some more. Then I went away to college and…"

He shrugged and tossed his head back, staring for a moment at the ceiling. "My family thinks I loved Sofia so much I've never gotten over her. That's the reason why I don't date. And I let them think it."

"Oh, Michael." Finn didn't mean it as an admonishment. He couldn't judge the man when Finn had hidden behind the grief of his parents' deaths.

Michael pressed their combined hands to his forehead. "It was a shitty and cowardly thing to do and it's over." He gave Finn the most earnest look he'd ever seen. "I want you, Finn. I think I love you. There's no more hiding. When you're feeling better, I'm going to take you to the North End to the best Italian restaurant I know. My aunt owns it, actually. I'm going to show you off to my family and friends and tell them you are what makes me happy. If they love me, they'll accept us both as we are."

Finn was shocked out of words, his head buzzed, not with the drugs but with the startling declaration. "Oh, wow," was all he could say.

Michael scrunched up his face. "Too soon for the L word?"

Finn shook his head, not caring that it made him

feel as if a ball bearing was rattling around his skull. "No, hell, no!"

They reached for each other at the same time. Finn won the race by clutching at Michael's shoulders and dragging him down to the bed. IVs clacked and monitors pinged. He didn't care. Michael Caruso loved him.

Epilogue

All those years of worrying and hiding, and it had been fine. The world hadn't come to an end, his aunt hadn't run him out of her restaurant, and no one had done anything worse than blink a few times when Michael had introduced Finn as his boyfriend. Of course, he'd told his parents first. Hearing through the grapevine that her son was gay would have been the real sin for Giada Caruso. It was something he'd had to do face-to-face, and it had gone fine as well. His parents were more open-minded than he'd given them credit for, although they were a bit disappointed he was dating someone who wasn't Italian.

They'd adjust.

It was a beautiful night, and with their stomach's full of Auntie's pasta, they strolled out of the North End holding hands. Michael was utterly happy and took a moment to appreciate that he was with the man he loved, who had fully recovered from his injuries. It was all a matter of clean-up now and there was no new case to fret over.

Pulling Finn in closer, Michael leaned over to give Finn a quick kiss.

Finn smiled back at him, but the smile didn't quite reach his eyes.

"What's wrong?"

"Nothing," Finn was quick to reassure him.

"I don't believe you. Did someone say or do anything tonight to upset you?" Just like that, Michael's mood shifted. He would bloody anyone who disrespected his man.

"No, no," Finn said, stopping and laying a hand on Michael's chest. "Everyone's been really nice. I love your family and can't wait for you to meet more of mine. It's just this place. I'm sorry. I'm killing the mood."

Looking around, Michael shook his head. "You don't like Columbus Park?"

Finn moved in for a hug. Michael held him tight and strained to hear the words muffled against his chest. "This is where they were killed."

Shit! He hadn't really known, he realized. You couldn't be on the force without hearing about how Callaghan senior and his wife were gunned down one night while walking the streets of Boston. The details got lost, however, in the telling.

"I'm sorry, baby, I didn't know." He kissed Finn on the temple. "We'll leave."

When he started to move, Finn held fast. "No, wait." He lifted his head up and scanned the area. "It shouldn't bother me so much."

"That your parents were murdered? Yes, it should."

"I mean this place. It's just a park. They're not here anymore and haven't been for a long time." He took a hard breath and pushed it out. "I wish we had an answer, the much vaunted closer. It might help to know at least who did it and why. I know Daire and Ronan look into it from time-to-time, as does Regan and her father before her." He looked up at Michael with a frown. "Still nothing. I can't let it go, and now that I'm on the force, I need to investigate it myself."

"We'll do it together. If there's something to find, we'll find it."

Finn gave him a smile that shot straight to Michael's cock. With Finn's injuries and the lingering memories of what the operation had been like, they hadn't yet slept together.

Michael cupped Finn's face with his hands and claimed his mouth with a long and lingering kiss. "Come home with me," he said when he finally came up for air. "I want you in my bed tonight."

"I'd like that."

****

The trip back to his place was as fast as Michael could make it. He vibrated with the need to take Finn in his arms and not let him go until they were both drained and boneless. He held back, however, determined to make this time special. Finn deserved that much and more, especially given the bizarre and even ugly circumstances of their only other time together. As soon as he had the locks secured on his front door, he swept Finn up into his arms and poured all his hunger into a kiss.

Finn was right there with him, his tongue pressing to gain entrance to Michael's mouth. Michael opened up for him and met him halfway. As their tongues wrestled with each other, Michael pulled them past the living room and into the bedroom. They grappled with each other's clothing as well until they were a tangle of half-naked limbs, knotted shirts, and stocking feet. They fell onto the bed together in that state, and neither of them could suppress the laughter when they flailed around to free themselves.

Michael used his superior size to pin Finn on his back so he could take control. Stealing the occasional kiss and nip and lick, he divested them both fully of their shirts and straddled Finn's torso. Then he worked his way down Finn's smooth chest, taking time to suck at Finn's nipples while his hands played up and down Finn's arms. Finn gasped and wriggled under the tame assault.

Pausing, Michael ran his fingers through Finn's hair and stared into his clear, blue eyes. "I want this to be our first time together. Forget what we did in the past, okay. This is me, Michael, making love to you, Finn. No one is here but us. No one will ever know what happened tonight except us."

Finn didn't laugh or blow off the idea. Instead, he looked at Michael with a serious expression and swallowed noticeably hard. "Yes," he said in a low voice thick with passion. "This is our very first time, and I want you inside me."

Michael's cock pulsed against his jeans, the confinement painful. It was so tempting to rid them both of their pants and dive into Finn's body. Michael wanted it hard and fast, but Finn deserved slow and easy. He gave Finn a lazy smile before returning to feasting on Finn's hard buds.

Within seconds, Finn writhed beneath him and urged him to go faster. "Damn, Michael, get on with it. Get me out of these pants. My dick wants to come out and play." He ended his scold on a moan when Michael's only response was to clamp his teeth on a nipple.

Slow and easy was still his goal. He'd get around to freeing Finn's cock, eventually. That was the plan until Michael found himself flying over and onto his back. Finn pinned Michael's arms with his knees before he could make a countermove. An evil grin spread across Finn's pretty face as he unsnapped his jeans and wiggled them down enough to free his hard dick and tight balls. It hovered like a tasty treat above his face. Michael opened his mouth without being asked.

Finn slid off his arms in order to slip his cock past Michael's lips. Michael sucked him as far as the angle would allow and took advantage of his freedom to run his hands up the backs of Finn's thighs. He cupped Finn's naked ass and squeezed before smacking one cheek with his palm. Finn jerked, sending his cock deep enough to hit the back of Michael's throat. Michael swallowed around the head while laving the underneath with his tongue.

With his head thrown back and his eyes closed, Finn moaned. The sight of his lover's pleasure thrilled Michael, pleased him as nothing else ever had. He urged Finn's hips closer with his hands as he raised his head to take more of him into his mouth. He sucked as he worked the cock with lips and tongue. Finn tried to twist his hips in reaction, but Michael held him firm, wanting to retake control.

"No, stop," Finn begged in a breathless voice. "I want to come when you're inside me."

Michael figured they could both get what they wanted. They had all night. Plunging his mouth down to the root of Finn's dick, he hollowed out his cheeks with a strong suck and threw in a fast vibrating hum at the same time. Finn came with a gasp. His cum shot down Michael's throat. Michael swallowed fast to keep up with the pulsing stream, then pulled back enough to be able to taste it. He wanted his lover's essence to linger on his tongue. He licked his lips with exaggeration as he let Finn slip out.

"God!" Finn collapsed sideways. "Fucker," he said without heat.

Michael grabbed his arms to help Finn land more gently on his back. He chuckled at the sight his lover made. Undone, satiated, eyes closed like he was going to sleep. Oh, no, none of that.

"That was round one, sweetheart," he said and began pulling the rest of their clothing off.

Finn lay passive, allowing Michael to pull him this way and that until they were both naked. Once that was done, Michael ignored his freed cock and went to work to arouse Finn once more. He started with Finn's knees, tickling the backs of them with his tongue. Then when he was satisfied he had Finn's attention, he moved up to the inner thighs, lapping and lipping each one until his lover was trembling with renewed interest.

The balls were next. Finn's sack was tucked tight against his body. Michael coaxed them down, sucking them into his mouth and rolling them around with his tongue. Finn groaned and fisted the covers beneath him. His hips writhed, and his cock showed signs of rising from its slumber. By the time Michael released Finn's balls, the cock was at half-mast. Michael's own dick literally wept with the need for attention.

Okay, he'd earned it, and Finn was about ready for round two. He reached into his bedside table and pulled out lube and a condom. It took no time to suit up for the game, so the next step was to make sure his guy was ready for him. A flash of memory intruded as he put a dollop of lube on his finger about how tight Finn was.

He pushed it aside. This was going to be the first time he'd feel what it was like to be welcomed into Finn's body.

"Fuck me, now?" Finn's eyes were half open as he stared up at Michael.

"All in good time, sweetheart. Let me open you up."

"I want it rough. You can do that for me, can't you, Daddy?"

Michael froze. "Why would you say that? Why would you call me that?" Was Finn trying to deflate his erection?

Finn grabbed the hand with the lubed finger. "Because we can't let what we had to do wreck any fun we might have with each other." Finn's gaze turned smoldering, there was no other word for it. "I like that you're older than I am. I want you to take me hard, to claim me."

Michael could only stare down at him. It wasn't right, was it? After everything they'd seen and done, surely this was the wrong fantasy to play out. So why was his dick still locked and loaded, all but jumping at the chance to slam itself in Finn's hole?"

"I'm a man, not a boy," Finn said in a seductive voice as he opened his legs and pulled them back. "This is a fantasy, not reality. A choice, not a job. Mutual desire, not exploitation. Come on, Daddy," he added as he pulled Michael's hand down. "Fuck me."

Michael hesitated for a second more before getting with the program. Finn was right. Roleplaying was hot and roleplaying with Finn was hotter still. He plunged his slick finger into Finn's hole and grinned when it caused the boy to arch his back and gasp. Finn was tight, but not so tight that Michael couldn't easily slide his finger in and out. He added a second finger within seconds and then a third. Each one ratcheted up Finn's response. The boy's dick was rock hard once more. Michael rewarded it by stroking Finn's prostate with each thrust of his fingers, making sure to press into it hard.

"Please, please," Finn begged as he thrashed his head from side-to-side.

"Please what, baby?" Michael teased as he shoved in his fingers.

Finn cried out, his hips bucking wildly. "Please fuck me, Daddy!"

Pulling out his fingers, Michael hoisted Finn's legs onto his shoulders and plunged his cock deep inside. They both yelled at the moment of joining, and Michael gave himself a second to simply feel. Finn's tight passage gripped his dick, milked it with quick pulses. Michael could imagine coming from that movement alone. But his baby wanted fast and hard, and that was what he was going to get. Michael gripped Finn's thighs, slid his cock out until only the head was still inside, then plunged it in again.

He set the hardest and fastest pace he could, slamming his cock into Finn's hole over and over. His chest heaved and sweat prickled his forehead. His slick palms scrambled to keep hold of Finn's swinging legs. He wanted to come, his balls practically screamed at him to go over the edge. He wouldn't, though, not until he'd pushed Finn over again first.

"Grab you cock, boy," he ordered, his voice choked with desperation. "Do it!" he yelled when Finn didn't comply. "Bring yourself off."

Finn jerked a shaky hand over to clasp his cock. He pulled in time with Michael's thrusts, and seconds later, twisted and flailed as he came again. The sight of it sent Michael over. He slammed his eyes shut and howled as the climax overwhelmed him. Hot ribbons of cum pumped through his convulsing dick, bathing it as he continued to thrust and try to deposit his semen deep inside his lover. He pulled Finn up tighter to him and ground their bodies together.

When his cock stopped pulsing, he collapsed on top of Finn. He barely had the energy to slide out carefully from Finn's hole and roll them both onto their sides.

They lay panting for long seconds, although Michael couldn't lie still. He petted Finn everywhere he could reach—hair, face, shoulders, chest. When he had enough breath to keep from passing out, he planted small kisses over those same spots.

With his eyes still closed, Finn chuckled. "You make me feel loved."

"You are loved," Michael confirmed by placing a kiss on Finn's mouth.

Finn's eyelids fluttered open. "I love you, too."

"Yeah?"

"Yeah."

"Good, I like that." Michael traced a finger along Finn's cheek. "How do you feel about having kids?"

Finn frowned. "I suppose I should have mentioned this sooner, but I can't get pregnant."

Michael blinked at the statement a few times before shoving a laughing Finn onto his back. "Seriously," he said, looming over him.

Finn sobered up. "Okay, seriously, I like the idea

of having kids—someday.”

"How about in the next couple of weeks?" Michael winced as he asked. He was about to drop a bomb on his new lover, and while it was a risk, this mattered to him almost as much as Finn did.

"What do you mean?"

"Remember that kid, Craig?" When Finn nodded, he continued. "They can't find a foster family for him, and his own family won't take him back. I hate the idea of his spending the next couple of years in a facility." Michael took a deep breath. "So, I've put in to be his foster parent."

Finn's eyebrows winged up, but he didn't say anything right away.

"I'm telling you, because we've got this amazing thing between us. I need to do this, but it obviously affects you. So, are you okay with this?"

Finn didn't answer the question, not with words. Instead, he bolted up and wrestled a startled Michael onto his back. He pressed his mouth to Michael's, his tongue entreating Michael's lips to part. Then Finn kissed him and kissed him and kissed him until both of their bodies stirred once more.

It was all the answer Michael needed.

Blue Heat

About the Author

I'm a corporate lawyer, happily married for over twenty years with three kids and four dogs. No white picket fence, but we do live in the burbs west of Boston. While my husband and I still do occasionally lick chocolate off each other, our more typical evening involves lying in bed once the kids are in theirs and reading separate books. Mine of course are romance. I started reading them as a defense against all those boring legal documents. Once I started, I couldn't stop.

I've also loved erotica since I was old enough to appreciate what sex is. I've been publishing erotic romance since 2009.

Besides my family, writing, and reading, my loves include the sight, smell, and sounds of the ocean (I'm a New England girl through and through), chocolate (naturally), prime rib (bloody), and good bourbon on the rocks.

Visit Samantha at
http://samanthacayto.com

To chat with Samantha Cayto and other Wild Rose Press authors of erotic romance, join us at www.groups.yahoo.com/group/thewilderroses.

Coming Soon

Double the Risk
Boston's Brave

by Samantha Cayto

Ronan Callaghan has finished raising his younger brother and is living life on his own terms. As a detective, he works the case of a murdered man with his new partner while helping his brothers dig into their parents' murder.

Diego Nieves is a transplanted New Yorker, looking for a fresh start after killing an underage suspect in the line of duty. Haunted by the event, he takes his job seriously but doesn't click with his cavalier partner, Ronan.

Cassidy Barnes is finally living the life she wants as an unattached medical examiner. She's determined to break old patterns and live life more fully by taking new chances. When two sexy cops catch her eye, her world turns upside down and she can't resist either men—the charming rogue or the serious romantic.

Ronan and Diego go from partners to rivals when they both seduce Cassidy. She struggles to choose between them. Keeping Cassidy could just mean Ronan and Diego will have to learn to work together.

Also Available

by Samantha Cayto

Catching Eagle's Eye
SEALs Going Hot

http://amzn.com/B00LW8316O

SEAL sniper, Dane Sawyer, is known as Eagle Eye for his deadly aim. He's also good at hiding his identity as a gay Dom. Childhood trauma has led him to live and play deep in the closet. Then a bullet to his thigh lands him on leave and in the incredible hands of a hot ensign assigned to get him back in the field.

Will Chadwick is happy to finally be living as an openly gay man in the Navy. And as a physical therapist, he's used to coaxing bad asses like Dane into doing their PT. Harder for him is resisting the temptation that Dane presents. He's a patient and hiding his sexuality. A prudent man would keep his distance.

But Dane doesn't know how to quit, and seducing Will has become a mission. The budding sub in Will can't resist the Dom's commands. If he could only make Dane see that being a man doesn't mean hiding his true self.

Catching Eagle's Eye

Prologue

"What the hell are you looking at?"

Dane started violently at his father's angry question. Oh, no, he'd done it again. He had lost track of where he was. He had let himself become distracted by the pretty pictures in his mother's clothing catalogue. It was lying right there on the living room table, impossible to miss. Impossible to resist. He had only meant to sneak a peek at all those nice men with their shirts off, with their pants off. He wasn't going to touch them even though his fingers wanted to trace along those hard lines of muscles. They looked just like their neighbor, Mr. Bennett, and he didn't look at him any more when he mowed his lawn. Dad had yelled at him for doing that and belted his backside good. These were just pictures. Why was it so bad to look at them?

Why was he so stupid? Why was he so wicked?

Dad grabbed his arm and shook him hard enough to snap his teeth together. "Answer me!"

Another shake forced an answer past his lips. Fear made him lie. "I was looking for pictures of ladies in their underwear, sir."

His father bent low, putting his face inches from Dane's. He cringed back at the look of fury and disgust in the older man's face. "Are you lying to me, boy? Those are pictures of half-naked men. Only queers look at other men. What have I told you about that?"

His breath hitched as he tried not to cry. Only babies cried, and he was twelve now. Dad said men don't cry, and he needed to be a man, not a baby anymore. If he let the tears fall, the punishment would be worse.

"I'm sorry," he choked out in a low voice. It was all he could manage and he knew it wouldn't be enough to keep his father from beating the "sissy" out of him. That's what his father called it when he slid his belt off his pants like he was doing now and slapped it against Dane's naked backside.

He would not cry; he would not cry! He'd take his licks like a man and never do this terrible thing again. But even as he said it, he knew he'd break his promise to himself. He couldn't help it. Something was wrong inside him.

The other boys kept talking about girls and breasts and stuff he didn't really understand. None of them talked about how nice it was to stare at the older boys with their tall bodies and strong muscles. Why couldn't he be like the others and stop doing things to make his dad mad? Not even the awful pain of the belt made him stop, not for long anyway.

"Looks like you're a little slow, boy. Your teachers think you're smart, but I know different. A smart boy wouldn't keep doing things that men don't do. So I'm going to give you another lesson with my belt, and by God, I'll keep doing it until you stop acting queer. Now, pull down your pants and bend over the chair."

Before he could do as his father commanded, a voice called out from behind him. "No, Cal, that's enough!" He turned to see his mother coming toward him. She was drying her hands on her apron, and her face told him she was mad, too. Mom never got mad. "You are not going to take a belt to him again."

"Stay out of this, Mary. You don't understand."

"Yes, I do." Her gaze flicked down at Dane. "I know he's curious in ways you don't like, and I don't like them, either. But beating him is not the answer."

"Then what the hell is? You want your son growing up queer?" He snapped the folded belt between his hands. The sound shot through Dane like a bullet.

"Of course not," she answered and there was a waver to her voice. Mom never argued with Dad. "We'll get him help."

"No." His father took a step forward. "No fancy shrinks that cost a fortune. I'll handle this."

"Cal, please."

"I told you to stay out of this, Mary. I'm the head of this household, and by God, I will be obeyed by everyone. Go back into the kitchen."

He saw it then, in his father eyes. If his mother didn't back down, his father was going to hurt her, too. Dane had never seen him do such a thing, but it was as clear as day that belt would land on more than his body if his mother didn't do as she was told. And when he looked at her, he saw the truth there as well. She wasn't going to go away. She wasn't going to leave him to the whipping he deserved. This was all his fault. His dad was going to hurt his mom because he couldn't control his dumb, sissy urges.

"No!" he cried as he launched himself toward his mother. She staggered backward, his body collided so hard with hers. Wrapping his arms around her waist, he looked back at his father with pleading eyes. "Please, Dad, no. Don't hurt her. It's me, just me, being bad. I'm weak. I'm being a sissy just like you said. But I won't do it anymore. I promise. Never again. I don't want to be a queer. I won't be one. I'll be a man, sir, I promise."

He drew a ragged breath, forced down his fear. "I'll be a man."

Chapter One

Dane stopped a couple of feet inside the therapy room and looked around, his right hand shoved into the pocket of his shorts and jangling his car keys. It was a large space with one wall of floor-to-ceiling windows creating a bright, cheery environment. Machines of various sorts were sprinkled around. A handful of wounded warriors were being put through their paces by what he assumed were physical therapists. Other than the clanging of weights and the occasional grunt, the most prevalent sound was soft voices murmuring encouragement and praise. He took everything in a single glance. He wasn't known as Eagle Eye in the Teams for nothing.

Christ, he so didn't need this right now. His boys were back in the thick of things, and here he stood waiting for some do-gooder to make his ouchy-boo-boo go away. He didn't need this kind of help. His leg was fine, mostly. Sure, he had a lingering limp when he allowed the pain to get to him. It was going to take time to strengthen the muscle and to brow-beat his limb back into submission. But he could accomplish that on his own. He wasn't like these other guys who were more seriously banged up.

A two-bit rebel soldier on a two-bit island nation had managed to make a lucky shot. The bullet hitting his leg was more like a gigantic mosquito bite than anything else. Given that he was one of the most successful snipers in the entire military, it was the embarrassment of being taken out by a rank amateur that caused him the real pain. A few days in the hospital and two weeks sitting on his ass at home and all was good, or at least good enough. He couldn't believe he'd been ordered to report for physical therapy here at Walter Reed. He was a SEAL, damn it all. He didn't need coddling.

There was no point in whining about the situation, however. That was also a pussy move, and he didn't play like that. He'd man up like he always did, follow orders, and get this thing over and done. Scanning the room once more, he looked for someone to check in with. He wasn't even sure who he was supposed to meet. He caught sight of some big guy sitting down on the floor with what was left of his legs straight out in front of him. The amputee wiped his hands across his eyes, probably clearing tears, the poor bastard. Dane tried not to stare. It was disrespectful, and it certainly made him feel stupid. By comparison, he had nothing to complain about, jackass that he was.

As he slid his gaze away, he caught sight of the man kneeling down on one knee in front of the patient and speaking to him in a tone too soft to hear. He saw a compact, muscular frame with copper-colored hair high and tight on top of a head he could only see in profile. His body responded instantly, forcing him to focus on the face. What he could see made him feel as if he were still out in the warm Maryland sun. A flush crept up Dane's cheeks as he stared at the angular face with a straight nose and a square jaw. The sight was compelling, and even though he was always careful not to pay too much attention to other men when on duty, he couldn't help himself.

The man finished what he was saying to the patient and placed a hand on the guy's shoulder in an obvious gesture of comfort. As if sensing the perusal, he turned in Dane's direction and looked him right in the eye. Dane felt that gaze square in his gut. Intense and boyishly handsome, the guy pinned Dane to the spot and robbed him of his next breath. It was a damn good thing he still had his hand in his pocket because it allowed him to push the fabric out a little to hide his thickening cock. Then the other man smiled as he stood and Dane had to stifle the little growl of desire bubbling to come out.

"Lieutenant Sawyer?" the man asked as he ambled over to where Dane stood staring stupidly back.

"Ah, yeah, that's me," he finally replied and shook the hand offered to him. Except he shoved his right back into his pocket because, shit, he was fully erect now.

Green eyes peeked out from long lashes. "I'm Ensign Chadwick. I'm going to be your therapist for the next little while." There was a pause in which Dane could have sworn he was being appraised by the other man and not in the strictly medical sense. "How's the leg?"

"It's fine." The response was automatic if a stretch of the truth.

Chadwick gave him a wry grin as if to say "yeah, right" without being insubordinate. "Mind if I have a look?"

Dane shrugged. "Sure."

Chadwick gestured toward a chair by the side of

the wall, and Dane took the cue. As he walked the few steps to the seat, his leg bitched at his steady gait. Damned if he was going to show weakness; he never did. Of course, that was just stupid thinking on his part given that the man he was trying to impress had access to his medical file and knew exactly what his condition was. Still, pride and all that.

He sat as the ensign bent down on one knee. The position was so like that of a submissive waiting for his master's orders that Dane's arousal kicked into overdrive. Oh, Christ, that was all he needed—visions of taking command of the earnest ensign and bending the sailor to his will. Yeah, those were appropriate thoughts to have on duty.

The bright overhead lights shone on the bent head before him. He could see slivers of blond threaded among the red. Shame the hair had to be kept so short. It would be beautiful in longer strands. He would be able to weave his fingers through them, grip and tighten his grasp until the guy moaned with pain. He'd use the grip to urge that pretty face forward to the space between his legs, coax those plump lips open to wrap around his cock. He could picture fucking that face in long strong strokes, his hard flesh swallowed down tight, wet heat.

Okay, he needed to shut down this whole train of thought before he came in his pants. Maybe he'd suffered a concussion and no one noticed. He needed to get right in the head the way he always did. He hadn't given his fantasies such free rein since, well, since he'd stopped being a punk kid who couldn't control his urges. It had been almost twenty years since he'd learned to hide his fascination with the male body.

What the fuck was the matter with him today?

Chadwick glanced up at him, and God, the man's eyes were intense in their compassion, which gave the illusion of arousal in Dane's overactive imagination. "I'm going to manipulate your leg now if that's okay with you, sir." As he asked the question, his hands hovered above Dane's ankle.

Dane coughed to clear the passion lurking in his throat. "Do whatever you need to, Ensign."

Chadwick answered with a quick smile before clasping the injured leg and sending a sharp pain up Dane's leg. Dane bit back the grunt desperate to escape and fixed his gaze across the room while his leg was lifted, pulled, and rotated. At least the discomfort helped to ease his hard-on. He might like to cause pain in his willing subs, but he was no masochist himself. Even when the therapist wasn't causing him to hurt, however, the touch of the other man had an equal, if opposite, effect. Those gentle fingers lit up his pleasure centers just as much as the pain ones. His cock responded with alacrity, so by the time Chadwick had carefully replaced Dane's foot on the floor, the erection was somewhat back.

"Okay, I'm done torturing you for the moment, sir."

Dane forced a casual nod of his head in response. "It was fine. I'm fine."

****

Sure, you are. Will could see the white lines of stress around his patient's eyes. God save him from the macho types who wouldn't admit to being in pain if their life depended on it. SEALs were the worst, always trying to pretend like everything was A-okay even when half a leg was missing. This lieutenant was the epitome of the damn-the-torpedoes types. Will could tell that from across the room. Tall and jacked with dark, wavy hair that was long enough to confirm the guy had been OCONUS, trying to blend in more with the locals even if his injury hadn't indicated his recent deployment.

It didn't take his Special Forces status, either, to tell Will that this was a man who took command. He could only imagine what being under Sawyer's control in bed would be like. God, this was his fantasy man, pure and simple, except this wasn't anything like simple. He was a patient and probably straight as an arrow. That boner he was throwing in his pants didn't mean anything, either. It happened to a lot of guys when they were being touched in ways that their bodies could interpret as erotic. It didn't mean anything. Nothing at all.

The intense stare was harder to dismiss, though. The officer gazed down on him as if assessing how tasty Will might be. The attention sent shivers down his spine, the kind that heated his blood instead of cooled it. Arousal stirred in his own pants, and he needed to head that off at the pass because a patient getting hard was one thing. You couldn't blame them, especially given the mental state of a lot of the people he treated. The therapist, however, was abso-fucking-lutely not supposed to be turned on by the person he was treating.

Of course, Lieutenant Sawyer wasn't his typical patient. His injury had left him in need of therapy, but he would fully recover in no time. No life-altering injury was clouding his judgment or making him vulnerable.

And now Will was trying to rationalize his reaction to the guy. Dumb and unprofessional and just the sort of thing the wingnuts would have a field day over given the repeal of DADT. He wasn't some oversexed pervert just because he was gay. It had been such a relief to be able to be open about his sexuality. Even though it didn't mean he had to be some paragon of virtue, he did owe it to himself and the guys he worked with to be professional. It would be the same way if he were straight, he wouldn't go around sprouting wood over a woman patient.

Falling back on the comfort of his standard routine with a new patient, Will put aside his wool-gathering about any attraction between him and Sawyer and outlined the process of evaluating what exercises would be appropriate for the lieutenant's injury. He stayed kneeling on the floor as he did so, and it seemed the most natural thing in the world to be at this man's feet and offering up his commitment to help him get back his full strength.

Sawyer simply sat, nodded, and grunted through the monologue to indicate he was listening. But his dark brown eyes told a different story. Still locked intently on Will's, they held promise of something exciting. Will couldn't keep back the blush that crept up his face. When he finished his usual spiel, silence reigned as the two men stared at one another.

"Excuse me, sir?"

Just like that, the connection between Will and the lieutenant was broken by the arrival of another therapist. Sawyer swung his gaze away in a bored fashion, as if he were waiting for a bus and looking for something to hold his attention. With an irritation that was unfair but real nevertheless, Will looked at the other therapist.

"What's up, Jenkins?" He tried to keep his tone pleasant. Given the way the other man looked at him, he wasn't so sure he had succeeded.

A clipboard was held out to him. "Would you mind taking a look at this new routine I have for Seaman Nieves?"

Oh, right, this was his job. He was supposed to be consulted by the more junior personnel. It wasn't Jenkins' fault that despite every intention to the contrary, Will had been acting as if he were trolling at a bar. Taking the offered document, he scanned the new therapy routine for a double amputee that wasn't making as much progress as they had hoped.

He nodded and returned it to Jenkins. "Looks good. We'll talk more about it later."

"Thank you, sir. Ah, sorry to interrupt." Jenkins retreated with a shy twitch of his lips.

"No problem," he replied and turned his attention back to Sawyer. "Sorry for the interruption, sir," he said in echo of Jenkins' apology. "I'm the senior therapist on duty so people consult with me on a regular basis."

The man shrugged and trained those intense eyes back on Will, although whatever he might have thought he'd seen in them earlier was gone. Instead of interest, there was resignation with a hint of impatience. Will knew that look, of course. PT was hard work, but for someone as used to being in the thick of action as a SEAL, the problem was undoubtedly more about how boring it was. Not a lot of fun came from cautious repetition intended to achieve results in a slow and steady fashion. The officer's response confirmed his thoughts.

"Let's just get this show on the road shall we, Ensign? I want to be cleared to go back in the field ASAP."

Standing up, Will said, "I understand, sir. I promise I'll get you back into shape as quickly as your body can tolerate."

Sawyer stood, too, and points for the macho man when he managed to hide the pain it caused him. It manifested in a mere twitch of one corner of his mouth. A less observant person would have missed it, but Will's job included knowing when to call it a day with a patient. Many of them tried to overdo, as if recovery could be sped up with sheer grit and determination. He had no doubt Sawyer would fall into that category.

Well, dealing with stubborn or aggressive patients was his specialty. So long as he could keep his focus on his job and off the fuckability of this particular patient, everything would be fine.

And, given how indifferent Sawyer was acting now, Will became convinced that any attraction he had sensed in the other man had purely been his own wishful thinking. Good. Great, actually. He had no illusions of recruiting straight guys to play on his team. Their relationship would be strictly professional.

"This way, if you would, sir." Will led the other man to the first piece of equipment he wanted to try.

Sawyer filed in behind him, and damned if it didn't feel as if those eyes were boring a hole through his back. His backside, actually. Ridiculous. Hadn't he just decided that there was no interest on the lieutenant's part? What an idiot he was being.

He needed to get laid, that was his problem. It had

been months since he had hooked up with anyone. He lived and worked in an area that was great for gay nightlife and, with his sexuality no longer a career ender, he could go out with impunity. He was off in two days' time. He'd go out and find some hot guy and get a hard ride.

When Will reached his destination, however, he turned to Sawyer and lost all train of thought. The heat in Sawyer's gaze was back, he was sure of it. It coiled its way around Will's throat, making it hard for him to breath, before slithering down to grab him by the short hairs. Blood pooled in his groin, and he knew a moment of terror as his cock twitched to life.

With extreme willpower, he held the arousal at bay and forced his thoughts back to the job. It took a couple of tries and a bit of throat clearing to find his voice and explain what he wanted his patient to do. Without a word and acting as if nothing untoward was happening, Sawyer lay down on the bench and started his exercise.

****

Sweat drenched Dane's shirt by the time his adorable torturer, aka Ensign Chadwick, took pity on him. Jesus Christ, how embarrassing to be so overtaxed by such simple exercise. He'd tried to keep up the façade of his leg not bothering him too much, but a few repetitions of the first machine had reduced him to grunts and groans. Less than an hour later, he panted as if he were in the middle of BUD/S training again.

Good thing none of his teammates were there to witness this pathetic showing. He was being a dick about it all, a real crybaby even though he was crying only to himself. Intellectually, he knew there was no shame in having been injured and needing PT.

Emotionally, however, was another story. Yeah, he was a real head case thanks to dear old dad, always keeping up the front of a tough guy.

Chadwick wasn't fooled, nor was he impressed with the macho bit. He had plastered a detached professional look on his almost pretty face while murmuring words of encouragement every miserable step of the way. He knew, too, when Dane had reached his absolute limit even before Dane realized it himself and long before Dane would have admitted it. Now, as he lay panting on a bench, he wondered if he had the strength to get up and leave.

Chadwick loomed over him. "How're we doing, sir?"

"Great," he lied because he was such a stubborn fuck and he couldn't help it. "I just need a minute."

As the understatement of the year hovered in the air between them, Chadwick grinned. "You did really well today, sir. I want to set you up on an every other day schedule to start. How does that sound?" To save himself further humiliation, Dane just gave a thumbs up. "To finish up the session, I want to massage the leg. Can you get up and come over to the massage table?"

The idea of the guy laying hands on his body perked Dane up considerably. Okay, it perked up a particular part of his anatomy, but fortunately Chadwick had already walked away so he didn't see Dane surreptitiously rearrange his cock as he stood up to follow. Damnation but his leg let out a yelp as he put his weight on it. Not limping was not an option, so he didn't even try. Besides, maybe he'd get a longer massage if Chadwick knew how much pain he was in.

Sure, that was a plan.

He lay face up on the padded table Chadwick motioned to and closed his eyes. When strong yet gentle hands curled around his calf, he allowed himself the luxury of relaxing into the sensation of being touched by another human being. There was nothing remotely sexual about the manner in which the therapist kneaded the sore muscles, all very professional. Still, his cock insisted on joining the party, hardening to a point that it tented his shorts.

The inappropriate reaction was mostly hidden under his T-shirt, but Dane couldn't believe Chadwick wasn't aware of it. He worked at keeping his breath even and focused on the sensations below his knee, some of which were painful enough to take his mind off fucking the body attached to those hands.

"It's okay, sir," Chadwick murmured. When Dane popped his eyes open, the younger man glanced down at the bulge and then back to what he was doing. "It happens to lots of guys when they're getting a massage. Nothing to be embarrassed about. Really."

Oh, yeah, right. Not a problem. "If you say so," he replied with a grunt.

Mercifully, Chadwick only smiled in response and dropped the subject for the rest of the massage. As painful as the therapist's strong fingers were, when it was over, Dane realized his leg didn't hurt as much. He was able to stand on it with almost the same level of discomfort as when he'd come in.

"Thanks," he said, taking a couple of tentative steps. "It feels better already." A simple lie, wishful thinking, really. "You sure we can't do this again tomorrow?"

Chadwick gave him a rueful grin. "Sorry, sir. Slow

and steady wins the race. If we rush it, we run the risk of making things worse."

"Right," Dane replied grimly. Without another word, he turned and left. The bright fall sun hit him right between the eyes before he had a chance to whip on his sunglasses. It was still early enough in the day that he was at loose ends. Until he was fit for duty, there wasn't much for him to do. Walter Reed was just far enough away from the SEALs' east coast base that he'd been ordered to bunk at one of the barracks on the hospital's grounds. That meant he couldn't make himself useful in any regard, nor did he know anyone to hang out with.

Getting into his jeep, he headed back to his temporary housing. He could have gone for a drive given that it was his left leg that was injured. Driving didn't hurt, despite command's insistence to the contrary. But he was too tired after the therapy session to risk it. The last thing he needed was a car accident, so he went back to the tiny space he called home.

He'd been lucky enough to be assigned a private room and had grabbed a cold bottle of cola from the barrack's fridge when he'd arrived. With more care than he wanted to need, he lowered himself onto the bed and took a long pull of his drink. The cold liquid slid down his throat and eased what tension was left in him after the soothing massage. His leg throbbed somewhat, but he ignored the feeling as he always did with discomfort.

Instead he allowed himself to think of Ensign Chadwick. The man was half tormentor, half tease. Okay, if you counted the teasing as a form of torment, then the guy was a complete torturer whether he intended to be or not. The idea of another man being the sadist was totally fucked up given that normally Dane was the one to inflict pain in a relationship.

Not that they were in a relationship, at least not a personal one. Chadwick had a job to do, they both did. Therapy would put Dane back in action, so he needed to focus on the guy's skills, not his desirability. Hard to do, though, when the very thought of Chadwick heated him up even while the drink worked to cool him down.

Kicking his trainers off, he lay lengthwise on the bed, propping his head against his arm in order to keep drinking. In this position, it was easy to see the hard ridge of his cock pressing against the worn cotton of his shorts. This is what Chadwick had seen during the massage, and Dane couldn't help feeling smug about the sizable package he displayed.

The few times he visited leather bars, he had worn tight pants to show off what he had to offer a willing sub. At eight inches, he had the right bulk to fill a sub's ass to almost painful fullness and drill it down hard. It was easy, too easy, to imagine Chadwick bent over a spanking bench, his bare ass glowing pink from Dane's hand, begging for more. His cock pulsed against its confines at the image. He allowed a moan to escape his lips before he took another swig of cola.

He tormented himself a few seconds more with the fantasy of smacking a willing Chadwick before he gave into the need to jerk off. Bottle in one hand, he unbuttoned his shorts and yanked down the zipper, taking his briefs with it. His needy rod sprang out, and he clasped it with a hard squeeze. With languid strokes, he caressed his dick, not caring that he had no lube. The harsh friction served him well enough. There was no willing sub at hand to hurt, so he might as well do it to himself.

He closed his eyes and pictured Chadwick spread before him, waiting to be filled. He ran his fingers over the hot flesh that still bore the marks of his dominion. The pink globes jerked and shimmied at the caress. Low moans washed over him. In his head, they came from his sub, though his own mouth made them.

"Please, sir," came the breathless plea.

"Please what?" he teased, knowing the answer already.

"Please fuck me." The ass wiggled in his hands, trying to entice.

Dane's breathing sped up. "I don't know. Have you been a good enough boy for me?"

"Yes, sir. I belong to you. I'll do anything to please you. My body is yours to command how you see fit."

"Ahh." Dane arched up into his own fist and stroked with greater urgency. He parted the imaginary ass cheeks to reveal the puckered hole waiting for him. Dusky and moist, prepped and ready. He rubbed the tip of his cock against the flesh before sinking it deep within the tight heat. He sighed with relief, his need partially sated simply by being encased by such a welcoming place.

For a few seconds, he savored the feeling before he gave into the need to thrust and pummel. His hips jerked with increasing speed as he pounded his body against Chadwick's. His perfect sub cried out in ecstasy each time Dane's cock filled him, meeting every thrust with a counter-one. Their bodies bounced against each other with a frenzy of movement.

Dane gripped his cock painfully and rubbed the

flesh raw as he climaxed through the fantasy. The bottle slipped out of his other hand when the force of his orgasm made him jack-knife into his fist. He grabbed his balls and squeezed. A loud roar sprang up in his mind, stifled because of the thin walls around him. But there was no one to see how his whole body jerked and shook. One final gasp pressed past his lips before he managed to lie face up once more.

In Dane's mind, Chadwick, still bent over, his body slick and shivering, looked over his shoulder and gave Dane a knowing smile. Shit. Dane shook his head to clear the image, but when he closed his eyes, it remained firmly fixed in front of him.

God damn! How was Dane supposed to get through PT with the guy now?

Also Read

Big Bad Easy

by

Ursula Whistler

http://amzn.com/B00EEEC2FE

A grueling unsolved murder case is the tipping point for detective Jameson Kelly. He's ready to hang up his holster for early retirement when Zara Robinson walks in to his precinct, the victim of a car break-in. She's everything Jameson likes in a woman—tall, blonde, beautiful and athletic. More than enough woman to take him down and make him beg for more. One more case can't hurt to help pass the time, especially one he knows he can solve.

Zara is a woman who knows what she needs, and top of her list is closure on this spree of car break-ins. And there's Jameson—he's big with an air of bad despite being a cop and all man. Man enough to easily make her feel soft and womanly. But when clues to the theft lead to something bigger, she's glad to have his brains as well as his skills on her side.

Thank you for purchasing this
publication of The Wild Rose Press, Inc.
If you enjoyed the story, we would appreciate
your letting others know by leaving a review.
For other wonderful stories, please visit our
on-line bookstore at www.wilderroses.com.

For questions or more
information contact us at
info@thewildrosepress.com.

The Wild Rose Press, Inc.
www.thewilderroses.com

Stay current with The Wild Rose Press, Inc.

Like us on Facebook
https://www.facebook.com/TheWildRosePress

And Follow us on Twitter
https://twitter.com/WildRosePress